CHILL TIDINGS

CHILL TIDINGS

Dark Tales of the Christmas Season

Edited by
TANYA KIRK

This collection first published in 2020 by
The British Library
96 Euston Road
London NW1 2DB

Cataloguing in Publication Data
A catalogue record for this publication is available from the British Library

ISBN 978 0 7123 5323 6
e-ISBN 978 0 7123 6742 4

Frontispiece illustration features art by Alfred Leete from *The
Sketch*, 2nd January 1907 © The British Library Board.

Cover design by Mauricio Villamayor with illustration by Sandra Gómez

Text design and typesetting by Tetragon, London
Printed in England by CPI Group (UK) Ltd, Croydon, CRO 4YY

Contents

INTRODUCTION

Two years ago I edited *Spirits of the Season*, an anthology of Christmas ghost stories that I found within the British Library's collections. With such vast collections to work with, it probably isn't too much of a surprise that there was an embarrassment of riches to choose from. This second volume includes thirteen stories that I wished I could have fitted into the first book.

The tradition of telling ghost stories on Christmas Eve was firmly established by the Victorian period. Its origins are in the early Christian belief that souls in purgatory were most active on the day before a holy day, and thus more likely to intrude into our world. Given that Christmas Eve night is one of the longest nights of the year in the northern hemisphere, it was also the perfect time to hunker down and enjoy the special kind of festive cosiness that you could only get from scaring yourself silly with spooky tales. However, in Britain there were also other reasons why short ghost stories gained such huge popularity in the nineteenth century. The industrial revolution also seemed to result in an increased interest in the supernatural – the more people knew about our world and could explain it, the more they wondered about what was beyond our ken, and unexplainable. More prosaically, the growth of the magazine industry, via improvements in public literacy (which created a new market) and printing technology (which enabled mass-production of reading matter for the first time) enabled the creation of periodicals filled with short fiction. Ghost stories, which were usually short and self-contained, fitted the brief perfectly. The British

Library holds hundreds of these magazines, from the nineteenth and early twentieth centuries, and there are sure to be more ghost stories waiting to be rediscovered.

The thirteen stories here date from 1868 to 1955. The earlier ones are all from fiction periodicals, while the later ones are from the period when magazines of this sort were on the wane, books were becoming cheaper and readers were more likely to get their ghost story fix from an edited anthology. The stories are written in a wide range of tone – there is traditional Victorian spookiness in 'A Strange Christmas Game'; a weird pagan vision in 'The Festival'; a sentimental tale of redemption in 'Old Applejoy's Ghost'. There are spooky monks, a Vampire lady, a fatal duel, a gruesome Father Christmas and festive gifts from beyond the grave.

The stories are arranged in chronological order with one exception. The final tale in the collection, by Jerome K. Jerome, is a comic take on the Dickensian ghost tradition, and was originally published as a novella. It is included here in full.

The ghost story is a genre of fiction that is both very traditional and frequently reinvented. The familiarity in the telling of spooky tales can also provide a wonderful source of comedy. It's rare to find a tradition robust enough to be gently – and self-knowingly – mocked and enjoyed in equal measure. I certainly hope the following stories will bring you as much pleasure in reading them as they brought me in selecting them for this volume.

TANYA KIRK
Lead Curator, Printed Heritage Collections 1601–1900
The British Library

A STRANGE CHRISTMAS GAME

Charlotte Riddell

FIRST PUBLISHED IN *THE BROADWAY*, JANUARY 1868

Charlotte Riddell (1832–1906) was born Charlotte Eliza Lawson Cowan. She grew up in a relatively wealthy Anglo-Irish family in County Antrim; her father was a flax and cotton spinner but was an invalid by the time she was born. When he died in 1851, his money passed to the family of his first wife, and his second wife, Charlotte's mother, received very little. Charlotte started writing fiction as a way of earning money to keep them both, and in 1855 they moved to London, where Charlotte's mother died a year later. In 1857 Charlotte married Joseph Hadley Riddell, a patent agent. She continued to derive an income from her novels and stories, as well as editing magazines, and she became the sole earner after her husband's bankruptcy in 1871. She died of breast cancer in 1906, having been supported in the last years of her life by grants from the Royal Literary Fund and the Society of Authors.

Although most of her work after her marriage appeared under the name Mrs J. H. Riddell, she also wrote under a number of pseudonyms and also sometimes anonymously. As a result it is hard to trace the full extent of her literary output, but it is large – driven by the financial burden she was under for most of her life. In addition to many short stories written for the popular periodicals, she also wrote novels. Today she is best known for her many ghost stories, some of which drew on the folklore of her native Ireland. As in this story, her ghosts often acted as agents of avengement.

W hen, through the death of a distant relative, I, John Lester, succeeded to the Martingdale Estate, there could not have been found in the length and breadth of England a happier pair than myself and my only sister Clare.

We were not such utter hypocrites as to affect sorrow for the loss of our kinsman, Paul Lester, a man whom we had never seen, of whom we had heard but little, and that little unfavourable, at whose hands we had never received a single benefit—who was, in short, as great a stranger to us as the then Prime Minister, the Emperor of Russia, or any other human being utterly removed from our extremely humble sphere of life.

His loss was very certainly our gain. His death represented to us, not a dreary parting from one long loved and highly honoured, but the accession of lands, houses, consideration, wealth, to myself—John Lester, Esquire, Martingdale, Bedfordshire, whilom John Lester, artist and second-floor lodger at 32, Great Smith Street, Bloomsbury.

Not that Martingdale was much of an estate as country properties go. The Lesters who had succeeded to that domain from time to time during the course of a few hundred years, could by no stretch of courtesy have been called prudent men. In regard of their posterity they were, indeed, scarcely honest, for they parted with manors and farms, with common rights and advowsons, in a manner at once so baronial and so unbusiness-like, that Martingdale at length in the hands of Jeremy Lester, the last resident owner, melted to a mere little dot in the map of Bedfordshire.

Concerning this Jeremy Lester there was a mystery. No man could say what had become of him. He was in the oak parlour at Martingdale one Christmas Eve, and before the next morning he had disappeared—to reappear in the flesh no more.

Over night, one Mr. Wharley, a great friend and boon companion of Jeremy's, had sat playing cards with him until after twelve o'clock chimes, then he took leave of his host and rode home under the moonlight. After that no person, as far as could be ascertained, ever saw Jeremy Lester alive.

His ways of life had not been either the most regular, or the most respectable, and it was not until a new year had come in without any tidings of his whereabouts reaching the house, that his servants became seriously alarmed concerning his absence.

Then enquiries were set on foot concerning him—enquiries which grew more urgent as weeks and months passed by without the slightest clue being obtained as to his whereabouts. Rewards were offered, advertisements inserted, but still Jeremy made no sign; and so in course of time the heir-at-law, Paul Lester, took possession of the house, and went down to spend the summer months at Martingdale with his rich wife, and her four children by a first husband. Paul Lester was a barrister—an over-worked barrister, who everyone supposed would be glad enough to leave the bar and settle at Martingdale, where his wife's money and the fortune he had accumulated could not have failed to give him a good standing even among the neighbouring country families; and perhaps it was with such intention that he went down into Bedfordshire.

If this were so, however, he speedily changed his mind, for with the January snows he returned to London, let off the land surrounding the house, shut up the Hall, put in a caretaker, and never troubled himself further about his ancestral seat.

Time went on, and people began to say the house was haunted, that Paul Lester had 'seen something', and so forth—all which stories were duly repeated for our benefit when, forty-one years after the disappearance of Jeremy Lester, Clare and I went down to inspect our inheritance.

I say 'our', because Clare had stuck bravely to me in poverty—grinding poverty, and prosperity was not going to part us now. What was mine was hers, and that she knew, God bless her, without my needing to tell her so.

The transition from rigid economy to comparative wealth was in our case the more delightful also, because we had not in the least degree anticipated it. We never expected Paul Lester's shoes to come to us, and accordingly it was not upon our consciences that we had ever in our dreariest moods wished him dead.

Had he made a will, no doubt we never should have gone to Martingdale, and I, consequently, never written this story; but, luckily for us, he died intestate, and the Bedfordshire property came to me.

As for the fortune, he had spent it in travelling, and in giving great entertainments at his grand house in Portman Square. Concerning his effects, Mrs. Lester and I came to a very amicable arrangement, and she did me the honour of inviting me to call upon her occasionally, and, as I heard, spoke of me as a very worthy and presentable young man 'for my station', which, of course, coming from so good an authority, was gratifying. Moreover, she asked me if I intended residing at Martingdale, and on my replying in the affirmative, hoped I should like it.

It struck me at the time that there was a certain significance in her tone, and when I went down to Martingdale and heard the absurd stories which were afloat concerning the house being haunted, I felt confident that if Mrs. Lester had hoped much, she had feared more.

People said Mr. Jeremy 'walked' at Martingdale. He had been seen, it was averred, by poachers, by gamekeepers, by children who had come to use the park as a near cut to school, by lovers who kept their tryst under the elms and beeches.

As for the caretaker and his wife, the third in residence since Jeremy Lester's disappearance, the man gravely shook his head when questioned, while the woman stated that wild horses, or even wealth untold, should not draw her into the red bedroom, nor into the oak parlour, after dark.

'I have heard my mother tell, sir—it was her as followed old Mrs. Reynolds, the first caretaker—how there were things went on in these self same rooms as might make any Christian's hair stand on end. Such stamping, and swearing, and knocking about on furniture; and then tramp, tramp, up the great staircase; and along the corridor and so into the red bedroom, and then bang, and tramp, tramp again. They do say, sir, Mr. Paul Lester met him once, and from that time the oak parlour has never been opened. I never was inside it myself.'

Upon hearing which fact, the first thing I did was to proceed to the oak parlour, open the shutters, and let the August sun stream in upon the haunted chamber. It was an old-fashioned, plainly furnished apartment, with a large table in the centre, a smaller in a recess by the fireplace, chairs ranged against the walls, and a dusty moth-eaten carpet upon the floor. There were dogs on the hearth, broken and rusty; there was a brass fender, tarnished and battered; a picture of some sea-fight over the mantelpiece, while another work of art about equal in merit hung between the windows. Altogether, an utterly prosaic and yet not uncheerful apartment, from out of which the ghosts flitted as soon as daylight was let into it, and which I proposed, as soon as I 'felt my feet', to redecorate, refurnish, and convert into a pleasant morning-room. I was still under thirty, but I had learned prudence in that very good school, Necessity; and it was not my intention to spend much money until I had ascertained for certain what were the actual revenues derivable from the lands still belonging to the Martingdale estates, and the charges upon them. In fact, I wanted to know what I was worth before committing myself to any great extravagances, and the place had for so long been neglected, that I experienced some difficulty in arriving at the state of my real income.

But in the meanwhile, Clare and I found great enjoyment in exploring every nook and corner of our domain, in turning over the contents of old chests and cupboards, in examining the faces of our ancestors looking down on us from the walls, in walking through the neglected gardens, full of weeds, over-grown with shrubs and birdweed, where the boxwood was eighteen feet high, and the shoots of the rosetrees yards long. I have put the place in order since then; there is no grass on the paths, there are no trailing brambles over the ground, the hedges have been cut and trimmed, and the trees pruned and the boxwood clipped. But I often say nowadays that in spite of all my improvements, or rather, in consequence of them, Martingdale does not look one half so pretty as it did in its pristine state of uncivilised picturesqueness.

Although I determined not to commence repairing and decorating the house till better informed concerning the rental of Martingdale, still the state of my finances was so far satisfactory that Clare and I decided on going abroad to take our long-talked-of holiday before the fine weather was past. We could not tell what a year might bring forth, as Clare sagely remarked; it was wise to take our pleasure while we could; and accordingly, before the end of August arrived we were wandering about the continent, loitering at Rouen, visiting the galleries at Paris, and talking of extending our one month of enjoyment into three. What decided me on this course was the circumstance of our becoming acquainted with an English family who intended wintering in Rome. We met accidentally, but discovering that we were near neighbours in England—in fact that Mr. Cronson's property lay close beside Martingdale—the slight acquaintance soon ripened into intimacy, and ere long we were travelling in company.

From the first, Clare did not much like this arrangement. There was 'a little girl' in England she wanted me to marry, and Mr. Cronson had a daughter who certainly was both handsome and attractive. The little girl had not despised John Lester, artist, while Miss Cronson indisputably set her cap at John Lester of Martingdale, and would have turned away her pretty face from a poor man's admiring glance—all this I can see plainly enough now, but I was blind then and should have proposed for Maybel—that was her name—before the winter was over, had news not suddenly arrived of the illness of Mrs. Cronson, senior.

In a moment the programme was changed; our pleasant days of foreign travel were at an end. The Cronsons packed up and departed, while Clare and I returned more slowly to England, a little out of humour, it must be confessed, with each other.

It was the middle of November when we arrived at Martingdale, and found the place anything but romantic or pleasant. The walks were wet and sodden, the trees were leafless, there were no flowers save a few late pink roses blooming in the garden. It had been a wet season, and the place looked miserable. Clare would not ask Alice down to keep her company in the winter months, as she had intended; and for myself, the Cronsons were still absent in Norfolk, where they meant to spend Christmas with old Mrs. Cronson, now recovered.

Altogether, Martingdale seemed dreary enough, and the ghost stories we had laughed at while sunshine flooded the room, became less unreal, when we had nothing but blazing fires and wax candles to dispel the gloom. They became more real also when servant after servant left us to seek situations elsewhere; when 'noises' grew frequent in the house; when we ourselves, Clare and I, with our own ears heard the tramp, tramp, the banging and the chattering which had been described to us.

My dear reader, you doubtless are free from superstitious fancies. You pooh-pooh the existence of ghosts, and 'only wish you could find a haunted house in which to spend a night,' which is all very brave and praiseworthy, but wait till you are left in a dreary, desolate old country mansion, filled with the most unaccountable sounds, without a servant, with none save an old caretaker and his wife, who, living at the extremest end of the building, heard nothing of the tramp, tramp, bang, bang, going on at all hours of the night.

At first I imagined the noises were produced by some evil-disposed persons, who wished, for purposes of their own, to keep the house uninhabited; but by degrees Clare and I came to the conclusion the visitation must be supernatural, and Martingdale by consequence untenantable.

Still being practical people, and unlike our predecessors, not having money to live where and how we liked, we decided to watch and see whether we could trace any human influence in the matter. If not, it was agreed we were to pull down the right wing of the house and the principal staircase.

For nights and nights we sat up till two or three o'clock in the morning, Clare engaged in needlework, I reading, with a revolver lying on the table beside me; but nothing, neither sound nor appearance rewarded our vigil. This confirmed my first ideas that the sounds were not supernatural; but just to test the matter, I determined on Christmas-eve, the anniversary of Mr. Jeremy Lester's disappearance, to keep watch myself in the red bed-chamber. Even to Clare I never mentioned my intention.

About ten, tired out with our previous vigils, we each retired to rest. Somewhat ostentatiously, perhaps, I noisily shut the door of my room, and when I opened it half an hour afterwards, no mouse could have pursued its way along the corridor with greater silence and caution than myself. Quite in the dark I sat in the red room. For over an hour I might as well have been in my grave for anything I could see in the apartment; but at the end of that time the moon rose and cast strange lights across the floor and upon the wall of the haunted chamber.

Hitherto I had kept my watch opposite the window; now I changed my place to a corner near the door, where I was shaded from observation by the heavy hangings of the bed, and an antique wardrobe.

Still I sat on, but still no sound broke the silence. I was weary with many nights' watching; and tired of my solitary vigil, I dropped at last into a slumber from which I wakened by hearing the door softly opened.

'John,' said my sister, almost in a whisper; 'John, are you here?'

'Yes, Clare,' I answered; 'but what are you doing up at this hour?'

'Come downstairs,' she replied; '*they* are in the oak parlour.'

I did not need any explanation as to whom she meant, but crept downstairs after her, warned by an uplifted hand of the necessity for silence and caution.

By the door—by the open door of the oak parlour, she paused, and we both looked in.

There was the room we left in darkness overnight, with a bright wood fire blazing on the hearth, candles on the chimney-piece, the small table pulled out from its accustomed corner, and two men seated beside it, playing at cribbage.

We could see the face of the younger player; it was that of a man about five-and-twenty, of a man who had lived hard and wickedly; who had wasted his substance and his health; who had been while in the flesh Jeremy Lester. It would be difficult for me to say how I knew this, how in a moment I identified the features of the player with those of the man who had been missing for forty-one years—forty-one years that very night. He was dressed in the costume of a bygone period; his hair was powdered, and round his wrists there were ruffles of lace.

He looked like one who, having come from some great party, had sat down after his return home to play cards with an intimate friend. On his little finger there sparkled a ring, in the front of his shirt there gleamed a valuable diamond. There were diamond buckles in his shoes, and, according to the fashion of his time, he wore knee breeches and silk stockings, which showed off advantageously the shape of a remarkably good leg and ankle.

He sat opposite the door, but never once lifted his eyes to it. His attention seemed concentrated on the cards.

For a time there was utter silence in the room, broken only by the momentous counting of the game. In the doorway we stood, holding our breath, terrified and yet fascinated by the scene which was being acted before us.

The ashes dropped on the hearth softly and like the snow; we could hear the rustle of the cards as they were dealt out and fell upon the table; we listened to the count—fifteen-one, fifteen-two, and so forth—but there was no other word spoken till at length the player whose face we could not see, exclaimed, 'I win; the game is mine.'

Then his opponent took up the cards, sorted them over negligently in his hand, put them close together, and flung the whole pack in his guest's face, exclaiming, 'Cheat; liar; take that!'

There was a bustle and confusion—a flinging over of chairs, and fierce gesticulation, and such a noise of passionate voices mingling, that we could not hear a sentence which was uttered. All at once, however, Jeremy Lester strode out of the room in so great a hurry that he almost touched us where we stood; out of the room, and tramp, tramp up the staircase to the red room, whence he descended in a few minutes with a couple of rapiers under his arm.

When he re-entered the room he gave, as it seemed to us, the other man his choice of the weapons, and then he flung open the window, and after ceremoniously giving place for his opponent to pass out first, he walked forth into the night air, Clare and I following.

We went through the garden and down a narrow winding walk to a smooth piece of turf, sheltered from the north by a plantation of young fir trees. It was a bright moonlight night by this time, and we could distinctly see Jeremy Lester measuring off the ground.

'When you say "three,"' he said at last to the man whose back was still towards us. They had drawn lots for the ground, and the lot had fallen against Mr. Lester. He stood thus with the moonbeams falling upon him, and a handsomer fellow I would never desire to behold.

'One,' began the other; 'two,' and before our kinsman had the slightest suspicion of his design, he was upon him, and his rapier through Jeremy Lester's breast.

At the sight of that cowardly treachery, Clare screamed aloud. In a moment the combatants had disappeared, the moon was obscured behind a cloud, and we were standing in the shadow of the fir-plantation, shivering with cold and terror. But we knew at last what had become of the late owner of Martingdale, that he had fallen, not in fair fight, but foully murdered by a false friend.

When late on Christmas morning I awoke, it was to see a white world, to behold the ground, and trees, and shrubs all laden and covered with snow. There was snow everywhere, such snow as no person could remember having fallen for forty-one years.

'It was on just such a Christmas as this that Mr. Jeremy disappeared,' remarked the old sexton to my sister, who had insisted on dragging me through the snow to church, whereupon Clare fainted away and was carried into the vestry, where I made a full confession to the Vicar of all we had beheld the previous night.

At first that worthy individual rather inclined to treat the matter lightly, but when a fortnight after, the snow melted away and the fir-plantation came to be examined, he confessed there might be more things in heaven and earth than his limited philosophy had dreamed of.

In a little clear space just within the plantation, Jeremy Lester's body was found. We knew it by the ring and the diamond buckles, and the sparkling breastpin; and Mr. Cronson, who in his capacity as magistrate came over to inspect these relics, was visibly perturbed at my narrative.

'Pray, Mr. Lester, did you in your dream see the face of—of the gentleman—your kinsman's opponent?'

'No,' I answered, 'he sat and stood with his back to us all the time.'

'There is nothing more, of course, to be done in the matter,' observed Mr. Cronson.

'Nothing,' I replied; and there the affair would doubtless have terminated, but that a few days afterwards, when we were dining at Cronson Park, Clare all of a sudden dropped the glass of water she was carrying to her lips, and exclaiming, 'Look, John, there he is!' rose from her seat, and with a face as white as the table cloth, pointed to a portrait hanging on the wall. 'I saw him for an instant when he turned his head towards the door as Jeremy Lester left it,' she explained; 'that is he.'

Of what followed after this identification I have only the vaguest recollection. Servants rushed hither and thither; Mrs. Cronson dropped off her chair into hysterics; the young ladies gathered round their mamma; Mr. Cronson, trembling like one in an ague fit, attempted some kind of an explanation, while Clare kept praying to be taken away—only to be taken away.

I took her away, not merely from Cronson Park but from Martingdale. Before we left the latter place, however, I had an interview with Mr. Cronson, who said the portrait Clare had identified was that of his wife's father, the last person who saw Jeremy Lester alive.

'He is an old man now,' finished Mr. Cronson, 'a man of over eighty, who has confessed everything to me. You won't bring further sorrow and disgrace upon us by making this matter public?'

I promised him I would keep silence, but the story gradually oozed out, and the Cronsons left the country.

My sister never returned to Martingdale; she married and is living in London. Though I assure her there are no strange noises in my house, she will not visit Bedfordshire, where the 'little girl' she wanted me so long ago to 'think of seriously,' is now my wife and the mother of my children.

THE OLD PORTRAIT

Hume Nisbet

FIRST CONFIRMED PUBLICATION IN
THE PENNY ILLUSTRATED PAPER, 22 FEBRUARY 1896
(VOL. 70, NO. 1813)

Hume Nisbet (1849–1921) was born in Scotland, the son of a house-decorator and his wife. At the age of 16 he travelled to Melbourne in Australia and worked there as an actor at the Theatre Royal, before travelling around Oceania more widely and returning to Britain in 1872. Before becoming a writer he tried to establish a career as an artist, and he did illustrate several of his own books and stories. He mainly wrote fantasy and adventure novels and stories, several of which were set in Australia and the Pacific, an area he visited twice more during his life. His entry in the Australian Dictionary of Biography states that he was outspoken on the subject of racism, and criticised the prejudiced treatment of Aboriginal Australians.

The first publication of this story is something of a mystery. Most sources state that it was published in a periodical in 1890, but the earliest I have been able to trace is February 1896 in London, followed by two printings in Australian newspapers later that year. In 1900 Nisbet included it in his collection *Stories Weird and Wonderful*. Although short, it's a powerful story of the Fin-de-Siècle period, and is akin to Oscar Wilde's *The Picture of Dorian Gray* and Bram Stoker's *Dracula*, the latter of which it predates.

Old-fashioned frames are a hobby of mine. I am always on the prowl amongst the framers and dealers in curiosities for something quaint and unique in picture frames. I don't care much for what is inside them, for being a painter it is my fancy to get the frames first and then paint a picture which I think suits their probable history and design. In this way I get some curious and I think also some original ideas.

One day in December, about a week before Christmas, I picked up a fine but dilapidated specimen of wood-carving in a shop near Soho. The gilding had been worn nearly away, and three of the corners broken off; yet as there was one of the corners still left, I hoped to be able to repair the others from it. As for the canvas inside this frame, it was so smothered with dirt and time stains that I could only distinguish it had been a very badly painted likeness of some sort, of some commonplace person, daubed in by a poor pot-boiling painter to fill the sec-ondhand frame which his patron may have picked up cheaply as I had done after him; but as the frame was alright I took the spoiled canvas along with it, thinking it might come in handy.

For the next few days my hands were full of work of one kind and another, so that it was only on Christmas Eve that I found myself at liberty to examine my purchase which had been lying with its face to the wall since I had brought it to my studio.

THE OLD PORTRAIT

Having nothing to do on this night, and not in the mood to go out, I got my picture and frame from the corner, and laying them upon the table, with a sponge, basin of water, and some soap, I began to wash so that I might see them the better. They were in a terrible mess, and I think I used the best part of a packet of soap-powder and had to change the water about a dozen times before the pattern began to show up on the frame, and the portrait within it asserted its awful crudeness, vile drawing, and intense vulgarity. It was the bloated, piggish visage of a publican clearly, with a plentiful supply of jewellery displayed, as is usual with such masterpieces, where the features are not considered of so much importance as a strict fidelity in the depicting of such articles as watch-guard and seals, finger rings, and breast pins; these were all there, as natural and hard as reality.

The frame delighted me, and the picture satisfied me that I had not cheated the dealer with my price, and I was looking at the monstrosity as the gaslight beat full upon it, and wondering how the owner could be pleased with himself as thus depicted, when something about the background attracted my attention— a slight marking underneath the thin coating as if the portrait had been painted over some other subject.

It was not much certainly, yet enough to make me rush over to my cupboard, where I kept my spirits of wine and turpentine, with which, and a plentiful supply of rags, I began to demolish the publican ruthlessly in the vague hope that I might find something worth looking at underneath.

A slow process that was, as well as a delicate one, so that it was close upon midnight before the gold cable rings and vermilion visage disappeared and another picture loomed up before me; then giving it the final wash over, I wiped it dry, and set it in a good light on my easel, while I filled and lit my pipe, and then sat down to look at it.

What had I liberated from that vile prison of crude paint? For I did not require to set it up to know that this bungler of the brush had covered and defiled a work as far beyond his comprehension as the clouds are from the caterpillar.

The bust and head of a young woman of uncertain age, merged within a gloom of rich accessories painted as only a master hand can paint who is above asserting his knowledge, and who has learnt to cover his technique. It was as perfect and natural in its sombre yet quiet dignity as if it had come from the brush of Moroni.

A face and neck perfectly colourless in their pallid whiteness, with the shadows so artfully managed that they could not be seen, and for this quality would have delighted the strong-minded Queen Bess.

At first as I looked I saw in the centre of a vague darkness a dim patch of grey gloom that drifted into the shadow. Then the greyness appeared to grow lighter as I sat from it, and leaned back in my chair until the features stole out softly, and became clear and definite, while the figure stood out from the background as if tangible, although, having washed it, I knew that it had been smoothly painted.

An intent face, with delicate nose, well-shaped, although bloodless, lips, and eyes like dark caverns without a spark of light in them. The hair loosely about the head and oval cheeks, massive, silky-textured, jet black, and lustreless, which hid the upper portion of her brow, with the ears, and fell in straight indefinite waves over the left breast, leaving the right portion of the transparent neck exposed.

The dress and background were symphonies of ebony, yet full of subtle colouring and masterly feeling; a dress of rich brocaded velvet with a background that represented vast receding space, wondrously suggestive and awe-inspiring.

I noticed that the pallid lips were parted slightly, and showed a glimpse of the upper front teeth, which added to the intent expression of the face. A short upper tip, which, curled upward, with the underlip full and sensuous, or rather, if colour had been in it, would have been so.

It was an eerie looking face that I had resurrected on this midnight hour of Christmas Eve; in its passive pallidity it looked as if the blood had been drained from the body, and that I was gazing upon an open-eyed corpse.

The frame, also, I noticed for the first time, in its details appeared to have been designed with the intention of carrying out the idea of life in death; what had before looked like scrollwork of flowers and fruit were loathsome snake-like worms twined amongst charnel-house bones which they half covered in a decorative fashion; a hideous design in spite of its exquisite workmanship, that made me shudder and wish that I had left the cleaning to be done by daylight.

I am not at all of a nervous temperament, and would have laughed had anyone told me that I was afraid, and yet, as I sat here alone, with that portrait opposite to me in this solitary studio, away from all human contact; for none of the other studios were tenanted on this night, and the janitor had gone on his holiday; I wished that I had spent my evening in a more congenial manner, for in spite of a good fire in the stove and the brilliant gas, that intent face and those haunting eyes were exercising a strange influence upon me.

I heard the clocks from the different steeples chime out the last hour of the day, one after the other, like echoes taking up the refrain and dying away in the distance, and still I sat spellbound, looking at that weird picture, with my neglected pipe in my hand, and a strange lassitude creeping over me.

It was the eyes which fixed me now with the unfathomable depths and absorbing intensity. They gave out no light, but seemed to draw my soul into them, and with it my life and strength as I lay inert before them, until overpowered I lost consciousness and dreamt.

I thought that the frame was still on the easel with the canvas, but the woman had stepped from them and was approaching me with a floating motion, leaving behind her a vault filled with coffins, some of them shut down whilst others lay or stood upright and open, showing the grisly contents in their decaying and stained cerements.

I could only see her head and shoulders with the sombre drapery of the upper portion and the inky wealth of hair hanging round.

She was with me now, that pallid face touching my face and those cold bloodless lips glued to mine with a close lingering kiss, while the soft black hair covered me like a cloud and thrilled me through and through with a delicious thrill that, whilst it made me grow faint, intoxicated me with delight.

As I breathed she seemed to absorb it quickly into herself, giving me back nothing, getting stronger as I was becoming weaker, while the warmth of my contact passed into her and made her palpitate with vitality.

And all at once the horror of approaching death seized upon me, and with a frantic effort I flung her from me and started up from my chair dazed for a moment and uncertain where I was, then consciousness returned and I looked round wildly.

The gas was still blazing brightly, while the fire burned ruddy in the stove. By the timepiece on the mantel I could see that it was half-past twelve.

The picture and frame were still on the easel, only as I looked at them the portrait had changed, a hectic flush was on the cheeks while the eyes glittered with life and the sensuous lips were red and ripe-looking with a drop of blood still upon the nether one. In a frenzy of horror I seized my scraping knife and slashed out the vampire picture, then tearing the mutilated fragments out I crammed them into my stove and watched them frizzle with savage delight.

I have that frame still, but I have not yet had courage to paint a suitable subject for it.

THE REAL AND THE COUNTERFEIT

Louisa Baldwin

PUBLISHED IN *THE SHADOW ON THE BLIND
AND OTHER GHOST STORIES* (1895)

Louisa Baldwin (1845–1925) was born Louisa MacDonald, the youngest of four daughters of a Methodist minister, and she and her sisters all went on to have notable domestic lives. Two sisters (Georgiana and Agnes) married artists (Edward Burne-Jones and Edward Poynter); the third (Alice) was the mother of the writer Rudyard Kipling. Louisa married the businessman Alfred Baldwin in 1845 and their son Stanley – who would later become Prime Minister – was born in 1867. Louisa Baldwin was dogged by ill health for much of her life, the cause of which has never been properly diagnosed, and spent a lot of time lying down in darkened rooms. As a result of her poor health she was largely released from the duties of running a household and one benefit was that she had more time to write. She had a successful career as a writer of short stories, and was a frequent contributor to magazines. Her ghost stories were collected into a volume and published in 1895. It is possible that 'The Real and the Counterfeit' had appeared in a magazine before this, but it may have been printed anonymously and I have not been able to trace it.

Will Musgrave determined that he would neither keep Christmas alone, nor spend it again with his parents and sisters in the south of France. The Musgrave family annually migrated southward from their home in Northumberland, and Will as regularly followed them to spend a month with them in the Riviera, till he had almost forgotten what Christmas was like in England. He rebelled at having to leave the country at a time when, if the weather was mild, he should be hunting, or if it was severe, skating, and he had no real or imaginary need to winter in the south. His chest was of iron and his lungs of brass. A raking east wind that drove his parents into their thickest furs, and taught them the number of their teeth by enabling them to count a separate and well-defined ache for each, only brought a deeper colour into the cheek, and a brighter light into the eye of the weather-proof youth. Decidedly he would not go to Cannes, though it was no use annoying his father and mother, and disappointing his sisters, by telling them beforehand of his determination.

Will knew very well how to write a letter to his mother in which his defection should appear as an event brought about by the overmastering power of circumstances, to which the sons of Adam must submit. No doubt that a prospect of hunting or skating, as the fates might decree, influenced his decision. But he had also long promised himself the pleasure of a visit from two of his college friends, Hugh Armitage and Horace Lawley, and he asked that they might spend a fortnight with him at Stonecroft, as a little relaxation had been positively ordered for him by his tutor.

'Bless him,' said his mother fondly, when she had read his letter, 'I will write to the dear boy and tell him how pleased I am with his firmness and determination.' But Mr. Musgrave muttered inarticulate sounds as he listened to his wife, expressive of incredulity rather than of acquiescence, and when he spoke it was to say, 'Devil of a row three young fellows will kick up alone at Stonecroft! We shall find the stables full of broken-kneed horses when we go home again.'

Will Musgrave spent Christmas Day with the Armitages at their place near Ripon. And the following night they gave a dance at which he enjoyed himself as only a very young man can do, who has not yet had his fill of dancing, and who would like nothing better than to waltz through life with his arm round his pretty partner's waist. The following day, Musgrave and Armitage left for Stonecroft, picking up Lawley on the way, and arriving at their destination late in the evening, in the highest spirits and with the keenest appetites. Stonecroft was a delightful haven of refuge at the end of a long journey across country in bitter weather, when the east wind was driving the light dry snow into every nook and cranny. The wide, hospitable front door opened into an oak-panelled hall with a great open fire burning cheerily, and lighted by lamps from overhead that effectually dispelled all gloomy shadows. As soon as Musgrave had entered the house he seized his friends, and before they had time to shake the snow from their coats, kissed them both under the mistletoe bough and set the servants tittering in the background.

'You're miserable substitutes for your betters,' he said, laughing and pushing them from him, 'but it's awfully unlucky not to use the mistletoe. Barker, I hope supper's ready, and that it is something very hot and plenty of it, for we've travelled on empty stomachs and brought them with us,' and he led his guests upstairs to their rooms.

'What a jolly gallery!' said Lawley enthusiastically as they entered a long wide corridor, with many doors and several windows in it, and hung with pictures and trophies of arms.

'Yes, it's our one distinguishing feature at Stonecroft,' said Musgrave. 'It runs the whole length of the house, from the modern end of it to the back which is very old, and built on the foundations of a Cistercian monastery which once stood on this spot. The gallery's wide enough to drive a carriage and pair down it, and it's the main thoroughfare of the house. My mother takes a constitutional here in bad weather, as though it were the open air, and does it with her bonnet on to aid the delusion.'

Armitage's attention was attracted by the pictures on the walls, and especially by the life-size portrait of a young man in a blue coat, with powdered hair, sitting under a tree with a staghound lying at his feet.

'An ancestor of yours?' he said, pointing at the picture.

'Oh, they're all one's ancestors, and a motley crew they are, I must say for them. It may amuse you and Lawley to find from which of them I derive my good looks. That pretty youth whom you seem to admire is my great-great-grandfather. He died at twenty-two, a preposterous age for an ancestor. But come along, Armitage, you'll have plenty of time to do justice to the pictures by daylight, and I want to show you your rooms. I see everything is arranged comfortably, we are close together. Our pleasantest rooms are on the gallery, and here we are nearly at the end of it. Your rooms are opposite to mine, and open into Lawley's in case you should be nervous in the night and feel lonely so far from home, my dear children.'

And Musgrave bade his friends make haste, and hurried away whistling cheerfully to his own room.

The following morning the friends rose to a white world. Six inches of fine snow, dry as salt, lay everywhere, the sky overhead a leaden lid, and all the signs of a deep fall yet to come.

'Cheerful this, very,' said Lawley, as he stood with his hands in his pockets, looking out of the window after breakfast. 'The snow will have spoilt the ice for skating.'

'But it won't prevent wild duck shooting,' said Armitage, 'and I say, Musgrave, we'll rig up a toboggan out there. I see a slope that might have been made on purpose for it. If we get some tobogganing, it may snow day and night for all I care, we shall be masters of the situation anyway.'

'Well thought of, Armitage,' said Musgrave, jumping at the idea.

'Yes, but you need two slopes and a little valley between for a real good tobogganing,' objected Lawley, 'Otherwise you only rush down the hillock like you do from the Mount Church to Funchal, and then have to retrace your steps as you do there, carrying your car on your back. Which lessens the fun considerably.'

'Well, we can only work with the material at hand,' said Armitage; 'let's go and see if we can't find a better place for our toboggan, and something that will do for a car to slide in.'

'That's easily found—empty wine cases are the thing, and stout sticks to steer with,' and away rushed the young men into the open air, followed by half a dozen dogs barking joyfully.

'By Jove! if the snow keeps firm, we'll put runners on strong chairs and walk over to see the Harradines at Garthside, and ask the girls to come out sledging, and we'll push them,' shouted Musgrave to Lawley and Armitage, who had outrun him in the vain attempt to keep up with a deer-hound that headed the party. After a long and careful search they found a piece of land exactly suited to their purpose, and it would have amused their friends to see how hard the young men worked under the beguiling name of pleasure. For four hours they worked like navvies making a toboggan slide. They shovelled away the snow, then with pickaxe and spade, levelled the ground, so that when a carpet of fresh snow was spread over it, their improvised car would run down a steep incline and be carried by the impetus up another, till it came to a standstill in a snow drift.

'If we can only get this bit of engineering done today,' said Lawley, chucking a spadeful of earth aside as he spoke, 'the slide will be in perfect order for tomorrow.'

'Yes, and when once it's done, it's done for ever,' said Armitage, working away cheerfully with his pick where the ground was frozen hard and full of stones, and cleverly keeping his balance on the slope as he did so. 'Good work lasts no end of a time, and posterity will bless us for leaving them this magnificent slide.'

'Posterity may, my dear fellow, but hardly our progenitors if my father should happen to slip down it,' said Musgrave.

When their task was finished, and the friends were transformed in appearance from navvies into gentlemen, they set out through thick falling snow to walk to Garthside to call on their neighbours the Harradines. They had earned their pleasant tea and lively talk, their blood was still aglow from their exhilarating work, and their spirits at the highest point. They did not return to Stonecroft till they had compelled the girls to name a time when they would come with their brothers and be launched down the scientifically prepared slide, in wine cases well padded with cushions for the occasion.

Late that night the young men sat smoking and chatting together in the library. They had played billiards till they were tired, and Lawley had sung sentimental songs, accompanying himself on the banjo, till even he was weary, to say nothing of what his listeners might be. Armitage sat leaning his light curly head back in the chair, gently puffing out a cloud of tobacco smoke. And he was the first to break the silence that had fallen on the little company.

'Musgrave,' he said suddenly, 'an old house is not complete unless it is haunted. You ought to have a ghost of your own at Stonecroft.'

Musgrave threw down the yellow-backed novel he had just picked up, and became all attention.

'So we have, my dear fellow. Only it has not been seen by any of us since my grandfather's time. It is the desire of my life to become personally acquainted with our family ghost.'

Armitage laughed. But Lawley said, 'You would not say that if you really believed in ghosts.'

'I believe in them most devoutly, but I naturally wish to have my faith confirmed by sight. You believe in them too, I can see.'

'Then you see what does not exist, and so far you are in a fair way to see ghosts. No, my state of mind is this,' continued

Lawley, 'I neither believe, nor entirely disbelieve in ghosts. I am open to conviction on the subject. Many men of sound judgment believe in them, and others of equally good mental capacity don't believe in them. I merely regard the case of the bogies as not proven. They may, or may not exist, but till their existence is plainly demonstrated, I decline to add such an uncomfortable article to my creed as a belief in bogies.'

Musgrave did not reply, but Armitage laughed a strident laugh.

'I'm one against two, I'm in an overwhelming minority,' he said. 'Musgrave frankly confesses his belief in ghosts, and you are neutral, neither believing nor disbelieving, but open to conviction. Now I'm a complete unbeliever in the supernatural, root and branch. People's nerves no doubt play them queer tricks, and will continue to do so to the end of the chapter, and if I were so fortunate as to see Musgrave's family ghost tonight, I should no more believe in it than I do now. By the way, Musgrave, is the ghost a lady or a gentleman?' he asked flippantly.

'I don't think you deserve to be told,'

'Don't you know that a ghost is neither he nor she?' said Lawley. 'Like a corpse, it is always *it*.'

'That is a piece of very definite information from a man who neither believes nor disbelieves in ghosts. How do you come by it, Lawley?' asked Armitage.

'Mayn't a man be well informed on a subject although he suspends his judgment about it? I think I have the only logical mind among us. Musgrave believes in ghosts though he has never seen one, you don't believe in them, and say that you would not be convinced if you saw one, which is not wise, it seems to me.'

'It is not necessary to my peace of mind to have a definite opinion on the subject. After all, it is only a matter of patience, for if ghosts really exist we shall each be one in the course of time, and then, if we've nothing better to do, and are allowed to play such unworthy pranks, we may appear again on the scene, and impartially scare our credulous and incredulous surviving friends.'

'Then I shall try to be beforehand with you, Lawley, and turn bogie first; it would suit me better to scare than to be scared. But, Musgrave, do tell me about your family ghost; I'm really interested in it, and quite respectful now.'

'Well, mind you are, and I shall have no objection to tell you what I know about it, which is briefly this:—Stonecroft, as I told you, is built on the site of an old Cistercian monastery destroyed at the time of the Reformation. The back part of the house rests on the old foundations, and its walls are built with the stones that were once part and parcel of the monastery. The ghost that has been seen by members of the Musgrave family for three centuries past, is that of a Cistercian monk, dressed in the white habit of his order. Who he was, or why he has haunted the scenes of his earthly life so long, there is no tradition to enlighten us. The ghost has usually been seen once or twice in each generation. But as I said, it has not visited us since my grandfather's time, so, like a comet, it should be due again presently.'

'How you must regret that was before your time,' said Armitage.

'Of course I do, but I don't despair of seeing it yet. At least I know where to look for it. It has always made its appearance in the gallery, and I have my bedroom close to the spot where it was last seen, in the hope that if I open my door suddenly some moonlight night I may find the monk standing there.'

'Standing where?' asked the incredulous Armitage.

'In the gallery, to be sure, midway between your two doors and mine. That is where my grandfather last saw it. He was waked in the dead of night by the sound of a heavy door shutting. He ran into the gallery where the noise came from, and, standing opposite the door of the room I occupy, was the white figure of the Cistercian monk. As he looked, it glided the length of the gallery and melted like mist into the wall. The spot where he disappeared is on the old foundations of the monastery, so that he was evidently returning to his own quarters.'

'And your grandfather believed that he saw a ghost?' asked Armitage disdainfully.

'Could he doubt the evidence of his senses? He saw the thing as clearly as we see each other now, and it disappeared like a thin vapour against the wall.'

'My dear fellow, don't you think that it sounds more like an anecdote of your grandmother than of your grandfather?' remarked Armitage. He did not intend to be rude, though he succeeded in being so, as he was instantly aware by the expression of cold reserve that came over Musgrave's frank face.

'Forgive me, but I never can take a ghost story seriously,' he said. 'But this much I will concede—they may have existed long ago in what were literally the dark ages, when rushlights and sputtering dip candles could not keep the shadows at bay. But in this latter part of the nineteenth century, when gas and the electric light have turned night into day, you have destroyed the very conditions that produced the ghost—or rather the belief in it, which is the same thing. Darkness has always been bad for human nerves. I can't explain why, but so it is. My mother was in advance of the age on the subject, and always insisted on having a good light burning in the night nursery, so that when as a child I woke from a bad dream I was never frightened by the darkness. And in consequence I have grown up a complete unbeliever in ghosts, spectres, wraiths, apparitions, doppelgängers, and the whole bogie crew of them,' and Armitage looked round calmly and complacently.

'Perhaps I might have felt as you do if I had not begun life with the knowledge that our house was haunted,' replied Musgrave with visible pride in the ancestral ghost. 'I only wish that I could convince you of the existence of the supernatural from my own personal experience. I always feel it to be the weak point in a ghost story, that it is never told in the first person. It is a friend, or a friend of one's-friend, who was the lucky man, and actually saw the ghost.' And Armitage registered a vow to himself, that within a week from that time Musgrave should see his family ghost with his own eyes, and ever after be able to speak with his enemy in the gate.

Several ingenious schemes occurred to his inventive mind for producing the desired apparition. But he had to keep them burning in his breast. Lawley was the last man to aid and abet him in playing a practical joke on their host, and he feared he should have to work without an ally. And though he would have enjoyed his help and sympathy, it struck him that it would be a double triumph achieved, if both his friends should see the Cistercian monk. Musgrave already believed in ghosts, and was prepared to meet one more than half way, and Lawley, though he pretended to a judicial and impartial mind concerning them, was not unwilling to be convinced of their existence, if it could be visibly demonstrated to him.

Armitage became more cheerful than usual as circumstances favoured his impious plot. The weather was propitious for the attempt he meditated, as the moon rose late and was approaching the full. On consulting the almanac he saw with delight that three nights hence she would rise at 2 A.M., and an hour later the end of the gallery nearest Musgrave's room would be flooded with her light. Though Armitage could not have an accomplice under the roof, he needed one within reach, who could use needle and thread, to run up a specious imitation of the white robe and hood of a Cistercian monk. And the next day, when they went to the Harradines to take the girls out in their improvised sledges, it fell to his lot to take charge of the youngest Miss Harradine. As he pushed the low chair on runners over the hard snow, nothing was easier than to bend forward and whisper to Kate, 'I am going to take you as fast as I can, so that no one can hear what we are saying. I want you to be very kind, and help me play a perfectly harmless practical joke on Musgrave. Will you promise to keep my secret for a couple of days, when we shall all enjoy a laugh over it together?'

'O yes, I'll help you with pleasure, but make haste and tell me what your practical joke is to be.'

'I want to play ancestral ghost to Musgrave, and make him believe that he has seen the Cistercian monk in his white robe and cowl, that was last seen by his respected credulous grandpapa.'

'What a good idea! I know he is always longing to see the ghost, and takes it as a personal affront that it has never appeared to him. But might it not startle him more than you intend?' and

Kate turned her glowing face towards him, and Armitage involuntarily stopped the little sledge, 'for it is one thing to wish to see a ghost, you know, and quite another to think that you see it.'

'O, you need not fear for Musgrave! We shall be conferring a positive favour on him, in helping him to see what he's so wishful to see. I'm arranging it so that Lawley shall have the benefit of the show as well, and see the ghost at the same time with him. And if two strong men are not a match for one bogie, leave alone a home-made counterfeit one, it's a pity.'

'Well, if you think it's a safe trick to play, no doubt you are right. But how can I help you? With the monk's habit, I suppose?'

'Exactly. I shall be so grateful to you if you will run up some sort of garment, that will look passably like a white Cistercian habit to a couple of men, who I don't think will be in a critical frame of mind during the short time they are allowed to see it. I really wouldn't trouble you if I were anything of a sempster (is that the masculine of sempstress?) myself, but I'm not. A thimble bothers me very much, and at college, when I have to sew on a button, I push the needle through on one side with a threepenny bit, and pull it out the other with my teeth, and it's a laborious process.'

Kate laughed merrily. 'Oh, I can easily make something or other out of a white dressing gown, fit for a ghost to wear, and fasten a hood to it.'

Armitage then told her the details of his deeply-laid scheme, how he would go to his room when Musgrave and Lawley went to theirs on the eventful night, and sit up till he was sure that they were fast asleep. Then when the moon had risen, and if her light was obscured by clouds he would be obliged to

46

postpone the entertainment till he could be sure of her aid, he would dress himself as the ghostly monk, put out the candles, softly open the door and look into the gallery to see if all was ready. 'Then I shall slam the door with an awful bang, for that was the noise that heralded the ghost's last appearance, and it will wake Musgrave and Lawley, and bring them both out of their rooms like a shot. Lawley's door is next to mine, and Musgrave's opposite, so that each will command a magnificent view of the monk at the same instant, and they can compare notes afterwards at their leisure.'

'But what shall you do if they find you out at once?'

'Oh, they won't do that! The cowl will be drawn over my face, and I shall stand with my back to the moonlight. My private belief is, that in spite of Musgrave's yearning after a ghost, he won't like it when he thinks he sees it. Nor will Lawley, and I expect they'll dart back into their rooms and lock themselves in as soon as they catch sight of the monk. That would give me time to whip back into my room, turn the key, strip off my finery, hide it, and be roused with difficulty from a deep sleep when they come knocking at my door to tell me what a horrible thing has happened. And one more ghost story will be added to those already in circulation,' and Armitage laughed aloud in anticipation of the fun.

'It is to be hoped that everything will happen just as you have planned it, and then we shall all be pleased. And now will you turn the sledge round and let us join the others, we have done conspiring for the present. If we are seen talking so exclusively to each other, they will suspect that we are brewing some mischief together. Oh, how cold the wind is! I like to hear it whistle in my hair!' said Kate as Armitage deftly swung the little sledge round and drove it quickly before him, facing the keen north wind, as she buried her chin in her warm furs.

Armitage found an opportunity to arrange with Kate, that he would meet her half way between Stonecroft and her home, on the afternoon of the next day but one, when she would give him a parcel containing the monk's habit. The Harradines and their house party were coming on Thursday afternoon to try the toboggan slide at Stonecroft. But Kate and Armitage were willing to sacrifice their pleasure to the business they had in hand.

There was no other way but for the conspirators to give their friends the slip for a couple of hours, when the important parcel would be safely given to Armitage, secretly conveyed by him to his own room, and locked up till he should want it in the small hours of the morning.

When the young people arrived at Stonecroft Miss Harradine apologised for her younger sister's absence, occasioned, she said, by a severe headache. Armitage's heart beat rapidly when he heard the excuse, and he thought how convenient it was for the inscrutable sex to be able to turn on a headache at will, as one turns on hot or cold water from a tap.

After luncheon, as there were more gentlemen than ladies, and Armitage's services were not necessary at the toboggan slide, he elected to take the dogs for a walk, and set off in the gayest spirits to keep his appointment with Kate. Much as he enjoyed maturing his ghost plot, he enjoyed still more the confidential talks with Kate that had sprung out of it, and he was sorry that this was to be the last of them. But the moon in heaven could not be stayed for the performance of his little comedy, and her light was necessary to its due performance. The ghost must be seen at three o'clock next morning, at the time and place arranged, when the proper illumination for its display would be forthcoming.

As Armitage walked swiftly over the hard snow, he caught sight of Kate at a distance. She waved her hand gaily and pointed smiling to the rather large parcel she was carrying. The red glow of the winter sun shone full upon her, bringing out the warm tints in her chestnut hair, and filling her brown eyes with soft lustre, and Armitage looked at her with undisguised admiration.

'It's awfully good of you to help me so kindly,' he said as he took the parcel from her, 'and I shall come round tomorrow to tell you the result of our practical joke. But how is the head-ache?' he asked smiling, 'you look so unlike aches or pains of any kind, I was forgetting to enquire about it.'

'Thank you, it is better. It is not altogether a made-up head-ache, though it happened opportunely. I was awake in the night, not in the least repenting that I was helping you, of course, but wishing it was all well over. One has heard of this kind of trick sometimes proving too successful, of people being frightened out if their wits by a make-believe ghost, and I should never forgive myself if Mr. Musgrave or Mr. Lawley were seriously alarmed.'

'Really Miss Harradine, I don't think that you need give yourself a moment's anxiety about the nerves of a couple of burly young men. If you are afraid for anyone, let it be for me. If they find me out, they will fall upon me and rend me limb from limb on the spot. I can assure you I am the only one for whom there is anything to fear,' and the transient gravity passed like a cloud from Kate's bright face. And she admitted that it was rather absurd to be uneasy about two stalwart young men compounded more of muscle than of nerves. And they parted,

Kate hastening home as the early twilight fell, and Armitage, after watching her out of sight, retracing his steps with the precious parcel under his arm.

He entered the house unobserved, and reaching the gallery by a back staircase, felt his way in the dark to his room. He deposited his treasure in the wardrobe, locked it up, and, attracted by the sound of laughter, ran downstairs to the drawing-room. Will Musgrave and his friends, after a couple of hours of glowing exercise, had been driven indoors by the darkness, nothing loath to partake of tea and hot cakes, while they talked and laughed over the adventures of the afternoon.

'Wherever have you been, old fellow?' said Musgrave as Armitage entered the room. 'I believe you've a private toboggan of your own somewhere that you keep quiet. If only the moon rose at a decent time, instead of at some unearthly hour in the night, when it's not of the slightest use to anyone, we would have gone out looking for you.'

'You wouldn't have had far to seek, you'd have met me on the turnpike road.'

'But why this subdued and chastened taste? Imagine preferring a constitutional on the high road when you might have been tobogganing with us! My poor friend, I'm afraid you are not feeling well!' said Musgrave with an affectation of sympathy that ended in boyish laughter and a wrestling match between the two young men, in the course of which Lawley more than once saved the tea table from being violently overthrown.

Presently, when the cakes and toast had disappeared before the youthful appetites, lanterns were lighted, and Musgrave and his friends, and the Harradine brothers, set out as a bodyguard to take the young ladies home. Armitage was in riotous spirits, and finding that Musgrave and Lawley had appropriated the two prettiest girls in the company, waltzed untrammelled along the road before them with lantern in hand, like a very will-o'-the-Wisp.

The young people did not part till they had planned fresh pleasures for the morrow, and Musgrave, Lawley, and Armitage returned to Stonecroft to dinner, making the thin air ring to the jovial songs with which they beguiled the homeward journey.

Late in the evening, when the young men were sitting in the library, Musgrave suddenly exclaimed, as he reached down a book from an upper shelf, 'Hallo! I've come on my grand-father's diary! Here's his own account of how he saw the white monk in the gallery. Lawley, you may read it if you like, but it shan't be wasted on an unbeliever like Armitage. By Jove! what an odd coincidence! It's forty years this very night, the thirtieth of December, since he saw the ghost,' and he handed the book to Lawley, who read Mr. Musgrave's narrative with close attention.

'Is it a case of "almost thou persuadest me"?' asked Armitage, looking at his intent and knitted brow.

'I hardly know what I think. Nothing positive either way at any rate,' and he dropped the subject, for he saw Musgrave did not wish to discuss the family ghost in Armitage's unsympathetic presence.

They retired late, and the hour that Armitage had so gleefully anticipated drew near. 'Good-night both of you,' said Musgrave as he entered his room, I shall be asleep in five minutes. All this exercise in the open air makes a man absurdly sleepy at night,' and the young men closed their doors, and silence settled down upon Stonecroft Hall. Armitage and Lawley's rooms were next to each other, and in less than a quarter of an hour Lawley shouted a cheery good-night, which was loudly returned by his friend. Then Armitage felt somewhat mean and stealthy. Musgrave and Lawley were both confidingly asleep, while he sat up alert and vigilant maturing a mischievous plot that had for its object the awakening and scaring of both the innocent sleepers. He dared not smoke to pass the tedious time, lest the tell-tale fumes should penetrate into the next room through the keyhole, and inform Lawley if he woke for an instant that his friend was awake too, and behaving as though it were high noon.

Armitage spread the monk's white habit on the bed, and smiled as he touched it to think that Kate's pretty fingers had been so recently at work upon it. He need not put it on for a couple of hours yet, and to occupy the time he sat down to write. He would have liked to take a nap. But he knew that if he once yielded to sleep, nothing would wake him till he was called at eight o'clock in the morning. As he bent over his desk the big clock in the hall struck one, so suddenly and sharply it was like a blow on the head, and he started violently. 'What a swinish sleep Lawley must be in that he can't hear a noise like that!' he thought, as snoring became audible from the next room. Then he drew the candles nearer to him, and settled once more to his writing, and a pile of letters testified to his industry, when again the clock struck. But this time he expected it, and it did not startle him, only the cold made him shiver. 'If I hadn't made up my mind to go through with this confounded piece of folly, I'd go to bed now,' he thought, 'but I can't break faith with Kate. She's made the robe and I've got to wear it, worse luck,' and with a great yawn he threw down his pen, and rose to look out of the window. It was a clear frosty night. At the edge of the dark sky, sprinkled with stars, a faint band of cold light heralded the rising moon. How different from the grey light of dawn, that ushers in the cheerful day, is the solemn rising of the moon in the depth of a winter night. Her light is not to rouse the sleeping world and lead men forth to their labour, it falls on the closed eyes of the weary, and silvers the graves of those whose rest shall be broken no more. Armitage was not easily impressed by the sombre aspect of nature, though he was quick to feel her gay and cheerful influence, but he would be glad when the farce was over, and he no longer obliged to watch the rise and spread of the pale light, solemn as the dawn of the last day.

He turned from the window, and proceeded to make himself into the best imitation of a Cistercian monk that he could contrive. He slipped the white habit over all his clothing, that he might seem of portly size, and marked dark circles round his eyes, and thickly powdered his face a ghastly white.

Armitage silently laughed at his reflection in the glass, and wished that Kate could see him now. Then he softly opened the door and looked into the gallery. The moonlight was shimmering duskily on the end window to the right of his door and Lawley's. It would soon be where he wanted it, and neither too light nor too dark for the success of his plan. He stepped silently back again to wait, and a feeling as much akin to nervousness as he had ever known came over him. His heart beat rapidly, he started like a timid girl when the silence was suddenly broken by the hooting of an owl. He no longer cared to look at himself in the glass. He had taken fright of the mortal pallor of his powdered face. 'Hang it all! I wish Lawley hadn't left off snoring. It was quite companionable to hear him.' And again he looked into the gallery, and now the moon shed her cold beams where he intended to stand.

He put out the light and opened the door wide, and stepping into the gallery threw it to with an echoing slam that only caused Musgrave and Lawley to start and turn on their pillows. Armitage stood dressed as the ghostly monk of Stonecroft, in the pale moonlight in the middle of the gallery, waiting for the door on either side to fly open and reveal the terrified faces of his friends.

He had time to curse the ill-luck that made them sleep so heavily that night of all nights, and to fear lest the servants had heard the noise their master had been deaf to, and would come hurrying to the spot and spoil the sport. But no one came, and as Armitage stood, the objects in the long gallery became clearer every moment, as his sight accommodated itself to the dim light. 'I never noticed before that there was a mirror at the end of the gallery! I should not have believed the moonlight was bright enough for me to see my own reflection so far off, only white stands out so in the dark. But is it my own reflection? Confound it all, the thing's moving and I'm standing still! I know what it is! It's Musgrave dressed up to try to give me a fright, and Lawley's helping him. They've forestalled me, that's why they didn't come out of their rooms when I made a noise fit to wake the dead. Odd we're both playing the same practical joke at the same moment! Come on, my counterfeit bogie, and we'll see which one of us turns white-livered first!'

But to Armitage's surprise, that rapidly became terror, the white figure that he believed to be Musgrave disguised, and like himself playing ghost, advanced towards him, slowly gliding over the floor which its feet did not touch. Armitage's courage was

LOUISA BALDWIN

high, and he determined to hold his ground against the something ingeniously contrived by Musgrave and Lawley to terrify him into belief in the supernatural. But a feeling was creeping over the strong young man that he had never known before. He opened his dry mouth as the thing floated towards him, and there issued a hoarse inarticulate cry, that woke Musgrave and Lawley and brought them to their doors in a moment, not knowing by what strange fright they had been startled out of their sleep. Do not think them cowards that they shrank back appalled from the ghostly forms the moonlight revealed to them in the gallery. But as Armitage vehemently repelled the horror that drifted nearer and nearer to him, the cowl slipped from his head, and his friends recognised his white face, distorted by fear, and, springing towards him as he staggered, supported him in their arms. The Cistercian monk passed them like a white mist that sank into the wall, and Musgrave and Lawley were alone with the dead body of their friend, whose masquerading dress had become his shroud.

OLD APPLEJOY'S GHOST

Frank R. Stockton

PUBLISHED IN *AFIELD AND AFLOAT*, 1900

Frank Richard Stockton (1834–1902) was born in Philadelphia, Pennsylvania, the son of a Methodist minister. He trained as a wood-engraver but became a hugely successful writer of novels and magazine fiction in the last two decades of his life. He is sometimes called America's first writer of science fiction, and was as well-known as his contemporary Mark Twain during their lifetimes. He struggled with his success, evidently feeling that the popular fiction he churned out for American magazines, despite providing him with financial stability, didn't allow him full creative independence. This story is sweet rather than scary, and features a very Victorian idealised Christmas.

The large and commodious apartments in the upper part of the old Applejoy mansion were occupied exclusively, at the time of our story, by the ghost of the grandfather of the present owner of the estate.

For many years old Applejoy's ghost had wandered freely about the grand old house and the fine estate of which he had once been the lord and master. But early in that spring a change had come over the household of his grandson, John Applejoy, an elderly man, a bachelor, and—for the later portion of his life—almost a recluse. His young niece, Bertha, had come to live with him, and it was since her arrival that old Applejoy's ghost had confined himself to the upper portions of the house.

This secluded existence, so different from his ordinary habits, was adopted entirely on account of the kindness of his heart. During the lives of two generations of his descendants he knew that he had frequently been seen by members of the family, but this did not disturb him, for in life he had been a man who had liked to assert his position, and the disposition to do so had not left him now. His sceptical grandson John had seen him and spoken with him, but declared that these ghostly interviews were only dreams or hallucinations. As to other people, it might be a very good thing if they believed that the house was haunted. People with uneasy consciences would not care to live in such a place.

But when this fresh young girl came upon the scene the case was entirely different. She was not twenty yet, and if anything should happen which would lead her to suspect that the house was haunted she might not be willing to live there. If that should come to pass, it would be a great shock to the ghost.

For a long time the venerable mansion had been a quiet, darkened, melancholy house. A few rooms only were occupied by John Applejoy and his housekeeper, Mrs. Dipperton, who for years had needed little space in which to pass the monotonous days of their lives. Bertha sang; she danced by herself on the broad piazza; she brought flowers into the house from the gardens, and, sometimes, it almost might have been imagined that the days which were gone had come back again.

One winter evening, when the light of the full moon entered softly through every unshaded window of the house, old Applejoy's ghost sat in a high-backed chair, which on account of an accident to one of its legs had been banished to the garret. Throwing one shadowy leg over the other, he clasped the long fingers of his hazy hands and gazed thoughtfully out the window.

'Winter has come,' he said to himself. 'And in two days it will be Christmas!' Suddenly he started to his feet. 'Can it be,' he exclaimed, 'that my close-fisted grandson John does not intend to celebrate Christmas! It has been years since he has done so, but now that Bertha is in the house, will he dare to pass over it as though it were but a common day? It is almost incredible that such a thing could happen, but so far there have been no signs of any preparations. I have seen nothing, heard nothing, smelt nothing. I will go this moment and investigate.'

Clapping his misty old cocked hat on his head and tucking the shade of his faithful cane under his arm, he descended to the lower part of the house. Glancing into the great parlours dimly lit by the moonlight, he saw that all the furniture was shrouded in ancient linen covers.

'Humph!' ejaculated old Applejoy's ghost. 'He expects no company here!' Forthwith he passed through the dining room and entered the kitchen and pantry. There were no signs that anything extraordinary in the way of cooking had been done, or was contemplated. 'Two days before Christmas,' he groaned, 'and a kitchen thus! How widely different from the olden time when I gave orders for the holidays! Let me see what the old curmudgeon has provided for Christmas.'

So saying, old Applejoy's ghost went around the spacious pantry, looking upon shelves and tables. 'Emptiness! Emptiness! Emptiness!' he exclaimed. 'A cold leg of mutton, a ham half gone, and cold boiled potatoes—it makes me shiver to look at them! Pies? there ought to be rows and rows of them, and there is not one! And Christmas two days off!

'What is this? Is it possible? A chicken not full grown! Oh, John, how you have fallen! A small-sized fowl for Christmas day! And cider? No trace of it! Here is vinegar—that suits John, no doubt,' and then forgetting his present condition, he said to himself, 'It makes my very blood run cold to look upon a pantry furnished out like this!' And with bowed head he passed out into the great hall.

If it were possible to prevent the desecration of his old home during the sojourn of the young and joyous Bertha, the ghost of old Applejoy was determined to do it, but to do anything he must put himself into communication with some living being.

Still rapt in reverie he passed up the stairs and into the chamber where his grandson slept. There lay the old man, his eyelids as tightly closed as if there had been money underneath them. The ghost of old Applejoy stood by his bedside.

'I can make him wake up and look at me,' he thought, 'so that I might tell him what I think of him, but what impression could I expect my words to make upon a one-chicken man like John? Moreover, if I should be able to speak to him, he would persuade himself that he had been dreaming, and my words would be of no avail!'

Old Applejoy's ghost turned away from the bedside of his descendant, crossed the hall, and passed into the room of Mrs. Dipperton, the elderly housekeeper. There she lay fast asleep. The kind-hearted ghost shook his head as he looked down upon her.

'It would be of no use,' he said. 'She would never be able to induce old John to turn one inch aside from his parsimonious path. More than that, if she were to see me she would probably scream—die, for all I know—and that would be a pretty preparation for Christmas!'

Out he went, and getting more and more anxious in his mind, the ghost passed to the front of the house and entered the chamber occupied by young Bertha. Once inside the door, he stopped reverently and removed his cocked hat.

The head of the bed was near the un-curtained window, and the bright light of the moon shone upon a face more beautiful in slumber than in the sunny hours of day. She slept lightly, her delicate eyelids trembled now and then as if they would open, and sometimes her lips moved, as if she would whisper something about her dreams.

Old Applejoy's ghost drew nearer and bent slightly over her. If he could hear a few words he might find out where her mind wandered, what she would like him to do for her.

At last, faintly whispered and scarcely audible, he heard one word, 'Tom!'

Old Applejoy's ghost stepped back from the bedside, 'She wants Tom! I like that! But I wish she would say something else. She can't have Tom for Christmas—at least, not Tom alone. There is a great deal else necessary before this can be made a place suitable for Tom!'

Again he drew near to Bertha and listened, but instead of speaking, she suddenly opened her eyes. The ghost of old Applejoy drew back, and made a low, respectful bow. The maiden did not move, but fixed her lovely blue eyes upon the apparition, who trembled for fear that she might scream or faint.

'Am I asleep?' she murmured, and then, after turning her head from side to side to assure herself that she was in her own room, she looked full into the face of old Applejoy's ghost, and boldly spoke to him. 'Are you a spirit?' said she. If a flush of joy could redden the countenance of a ghost, his face would have glowed like sunlit rose. 'Dear child,' he exclaimed, 'I am the ghost of your uncle's grandfather. His younger sister, Maria, was your mother, and therefore, I am the ghost of your great-grandfather.'

'Then you must be the original Applejoy,' said Bertha, 'and I think it very wonderful that I am not afraid of you. You look as if you would not hurt anybody in this world, especially me!'

'There you have it, my dear!' he exclaimed, bringing his cane down upon the floor with a violence which had it been the cane it used to be would have wakened everybody in the house. 'I vow to you there is not a person in the world for whom I have such an affection as I feel for you. You have brought into this house something of the old life. I wish I could tell you how happy I have been since the bright spring day that brought you here.'

'I did not suppose I would make anyone happy by coming here,' said Bertha. 'Uncle John does not seem to care much about me, and I did not know about you.'

'No, indeed,' exclaimed the good ghost, 'you did not know about me, but you will. First, however, we must get down to business. I came here tonight with a special object. It is about Christmas. Your uncle does not mean to have any Christmas in this house, but I intend, if I can possibly do so, to prevent him from disgracing himself. Still, I cannot do anything without help, and there is nobody to help me but you. Will you do it?'

Bertha could not refrain from a smile. 'It would be funny to help a ghost,' she said, 'but if I can assist you I shall be very glad.'

'I want you to go into the lower part of the house,' said he. 'I have something to show you. I shall go down and wait for you. Dress yourself as warmly as you can, and have you some soft slippers that will make no noise?'

'Oh, yes,' said Bertha, her eyes twinkling with delight. 'I shall be dressed and with you in no time.'

'Do not hurry yourself,' said the good ghost as he left the room 'We have most of the night before us.'

When the young girl had descended the great staircase almost as noiselessly as the ghost, she found her venerable companion waiting for her. 'Do you see the lantern on the table?' said he. 'John uses it when he goes his round of the house at bedtime. There are matches hanging above it. Please light it. You may be sure I would not put you to this trouble if I were able to do it myself.'

When she had lighted the brass lantern, the ghost invited her to enter the study. 'Now,' said he as he led the way to the large desk with the cabinet above it, 'will you be so good as to open that glass door and put your hand into the front corner of that middle shelf? You will feel a key hanging upon a little hook.'

'But this is my uncle's cabinet,' Bertha said, 'and I have no right to meddle with his keys and things!'

The ghost drew himself up to the six feet two inches which had been his stature in life. 'This was my cabinet,' he said, 'and I have never surrendered it to your uncle John! With my own hands I screwed the little hook into that dark corner and hung the key upon it! Now I beg you to take down that key and unlock that little drawer at the bottom.'

Without a moment's hesitation Bertha took the key from the hook unlocked and opened the drawer. 'It is full of old keys all tied together in a bunch!' she said.

'Yes,' said the ghost. 'Now, my dear, I want you to understand that what we are going to do is strictly correct and proper. This was once my house—everything in it I planned and arranged. I am now going to take you into the cellars of my old mansion. They are wonderful cellars; they were my pride and glory! Are you afraid,' he said, 'to descend with me into these subterranean regions?'

'Not a bit!' exclaimed Bertha. 'I think it will be the jolliest thing in the world to go with my great-grandfather into the cellars which he built himself, and of which he was so proud.'

This speech so charmed the ghost of old Applejoy that he would instantly have kissed his great-granddaughter had it not been that he was afraid of giving her a cold.

'You are a girl to my liking!' he exclaimed. 'I wish you had been living at the time I was alive and master of this house. We should have had gay times together!'

'I wish you were alive now, dear Great-grandpapa,' said she. 'Let us go on—I am all impatience!'

They then descended into the cellars, which, until the present owner came into possession of the estate, had been famous throughout the neighbourhood. 'This way,' said old Applejoy's ghost. 'Do you see that row of old casks nearly covered with cobwebs and dust? They contain some of the choicest spirits ever brought into this country, rum from Jamaica, brandy from France, port and Madeira.

'Come into this little room. Now, then, hold up your lantern. Notice that row of glass jars on the shelf. They are filled with the finest mincemeat ever made and just as good as it ever was! And there are a lot more jars and cans all tightly sealed. I do not know what good things are in them, but I am sure their contents are just what will be wanted to fill out a Christmas table.

'Now, my dear, I want to show you the grandest thing in these cellars. Behold that wooden box! Inside it is an airtight box made of tin. Inside that is a great plum cake put into that box by me! I intended it to stay there for a long time, for plum cake gets better and better the longer it is kept. The people who eat that cake, my dear Bertha, will be blessed above all their fellow mortals!

'And now I think you have seen enough to understand thoroughly that these cellars are the abode of many good things to eat and to drink. It is their abode, but if John could have his way it would be their sepulchre!'

'But why did you bring me here, Great-grandpapa?' said Bertha. 'Do you want me to come down here and have my Christmas dinner with you?'

'No, indeed,' said old Applejoy's ghost. 'Come upstairs, and let us go into the study.' Once they were there, Bertha sat down before the fireplace and warmed her fingers over the few embers it contained.

'Bertha,' said the spirit of her great-grandfather, 'it is wicked not to celebrate Christmas, especially when one is able to do so in the most hospitable and generous way. For years John has taken no notice of Christmas, and it is our duty to reform him if we can! There is not much time before Christmas Day, but there is time enough to do everything that has to be done, if you and I go to work and set other people to work.'

'And how are we to do that?' asked Bertha.

'The straightforward thing to do,' said the ghost, 'is for me to appear to your uncle, tell him his duty, and urge him to perform it, but I know what will be the result. He would call the interview a dream. But there is nothing dreamlike about you, my dear. If anyone hears you talking he will know he is awake.'

'Do you want me to talk to Uncle?' said Bertha, smiling.

'Yes,' said old Applejoy's ghost. 'I want you to go to him immediately after breakfast tomorrow morning and tell him exactly what has happened this night; about the casks of spirits, the jars of mincemeat, and the wooden box nailed fast and tight with the tin box inside holding the plum cake. John knows all about that cake, and he knows all about me, too.'

'And what is the message?' asked Bertha.

'It is simply this,' said the ghost. 'When you have told him all the events of this night, and when he sees that they must have happened, I want you to tell him that it is the wish and desire of his grandfather, to whom he owes everything, that there shall be worthy festivities in this house on Christmas Day and Night. Tell him to open his cellars and spend his money. Tell him to send for at least a dozen good friends and relatives to attend the great holiday celebration that is to be held in this house.

'Now, my dear,' said old Applejoy's ghost, drawing near to the young girl, 'I want to ask you—a private, personal question. Who is Tom?'

At these words a sudden blush rushed into the cheeks of Bertha. 'Tom?' she said. 'What Tom?'

'I am sure you know a young man named Tom, and I want you to tell me who he is. My name was Tom, and I am very fond of Toms. Is he a nice young fellow? Do you like him very much?'

'Yes,' said Bertha, meaning the answer to cover both questions.

'And does he like you?'

'I think so,' said Bertha.

'That means you are in love with each other!' exclaimed old Applejoy's ghost. 'And now, my dear, tell me his last name. Out with it!'

'Mr. Burcham,' said Bertha, her cheeks now a little pale.

'Son of Thomas Burcham of the Meadows?'

'Yes, sir,' said Bertha.

The ghost of old Applejoy gazed down upon his great-granddaughter with pride and admiration. 'My dear Bertha,' he exclaimed, 'I congratulate you! I have seen young Tom. He is a fine-looking fellow, and if you love him I know he is a good one. Now, I'll tell you what we will do, Bertha. We will have Tom here on Christmas.'

'Oh, Great-grandfather, I can't ask Uncle to invite him!' she exclaimed.

'We will have a bigger party than we thought we would,' said the beaming ghost. 'All the invited guests will be asked to bring their families. When a big dinner is given at this house, Thomas Burcham, Sr., must not be left out, and he is bound to bring Tom. Now skip back to your bed, and immediately after breakfast come here to your uncle and tell him everything I have told you to tell him.'

Bertha hesitated. 'Great-grandfather,' she said, 'if Uncle does allow us to celebrate Christmas, will you be with us?'

'Yes, indeed, my dear,' said he. 'And you need not be afraid of my frightening anybody. I shall be everywhere and I shall hear everything, but I shall be visible only to the loveliest woman who ever graced this mansion. And now be off to bed without another word.'

'If she hadn't gone,' said old Applejoy's ghost to himself, 'I couldn't have helped giving her a good-night kiss.'

The next morning, as Bertha told the story of her night's adventures to her uncle, the face of John Applejoy grew paler and paler. He was a hard-headed man, but a superstitious one, and when Bertha told him of his grandfather's plum cake, the existence of which he had believed was not known to anyone but himself, he felt it was impossible for the girl to have dreamed these things. With all the power of his will he opposed this belief, but it was too much for him, and he surrendered. But he was a proud man and would not admit to his niece that he put any faith in the existence of ghosts.

'My dear,' said he, rising, his face still pale, but his expression under good control, 'although there is nothing of weight in what you have told me—for traditions about my cellars have been afloat in the family—still your pretty little story suggests something to me. This is Christmastime and I had almost overlooked it. You are young and lively and accustomed to the celebration of holidays. Therefore, I have determined, my dear, to have a grand Christmas dinner and invite our friends and their families. I know there must be good things in the cellars, although I had almost forgotten them, and they shall be brought up and spread out and enjoyed. Now go and send Mrs. Dipperton to me, and when we have finished our consultation, you and I will make out a list of guests.'

When she had gone, John Applejoy sat down in his big chair and looked fixedly into the fire. He would not have dared to go to bed that night if he had disregarded the message from his grandfather.

Never had there been such a glorious Christmastime within the walls of the old house. The news that old Mr. Applejoy was sending out invitations to a Christmas dinner spread like wildfire through the neighbourhood. The idea of inviting people by families was considered a grand one, worthy indeed of the times of old Mr. Tom Applejoy, the grandfather of the present owner, who had been the most hospitable man in the whole country.

For the first time in nearly a century all the leaves of the great dining table were put into use, and the table had as much as it could do to stand up under its burdens brought from cellar, barn, and surrounding country. In the very middle of everything was the wonderful plum cake which had been put away by the famous grandfather of the host.

But the cake was not cut. 'My friends,' said Mr. John Applejoy, 'we may all look at this cake but we will not eat it! We will keep it just as it is until a marriage shall occur in this family. Then you are all invited to come and enjoy it!'

At the conclusion of this little speech old Applejoy's ghost patted his grandson upon the head. 'You don't feel that, John,' he said to himself, 'but it is approbation, and this is the first time I have ever approved of you!'

Late in the evening there was a grand dance in the great hall, which opened with an old-fashioned minuet, and when the merry guests were forming on the floor, a young man named Tom came forward and asked the hand of Bertha.

'No,' said she, 'not this time. I am going to dance this first dance with—well, we will say by myself!'

At these words the most thoroughly gratified ghost in all space stepped up to the side of the lovely girl, and with his cocked hat folded flat under his left arm, he made a low bow and held out his hand. With his long waistcoat trimmed with lace, his tightly drawn stockings and his buckled shoes, there was not such a gallant figure in the whole company.

Bertha put out her hand and touched the shadowy fingers of her partner, and then, side by side, she and the ghost of her great-grandfather opened the ball. With all the grace of fresh young beauty and ancient courtliness they danced the minuet.

'What a strange young girl,' said some of the guests, 'to go through that dance all by herself, but how beautifully she did it!'

'Very eccentric, my dear!' said Mr. John Applejoy when the dance was over. 'But I could not help thinking as I looked at you that there was nobody in this room that was worthy to be your partner.'

'You are wrong there, old fellow!' was the simultaneous mental ejaculation of young Tom Burcham and of old Applejoy's ghost.

TRANSITION

Algernon Blackwood

FIRST PUBLISHED IN *THE NEW WITNESS*, 11
DECEMBER 1913 (VOL. 3, NO. 58)

Algernon Henry Blackwood (1869–1951) established a new kind of weird fiction, describing supernatural encounters in which the natural world possesses sinister powers. He was born into a wealthy family, the son of a man who had been a playboy known as 'Beauty Blackwood' but who had been converted into a deeply conservative and evangelical Christian during the Crimean War. Blackwood rebelled against his upbringing, becoming interested in mysticism and involved in The Hermetic Order of the Golden Dawn, an occult group that also included Bram Stoker, Arthur Machen and Aleister Crowley as members.

In addition to fiction in which he explored the natural world as the source of a dark, mystical force, Blackwood was famed for ghost stories. He featured on the BBC's first ever television programme, *Picture Page*, telling a ghost story at the broadcast from Alexandra Palace on 2 November 1936. He later made regular appearances on both television and radio, and became known as 'The Ghost Man'.

J ohn Mudbury was on his way home from the shops, his arms full of Christmas Presents. It was after six o'clock and the streets were very crowded. He was an ordinary man, lived in an ordinary suburban flat, with an ordinary wife and ordinary children. He did not think them ordinary, but everybody else did. He had ordinary presents for each one, a cheap blotter for his wife, a cheap air-gun for the boy, and so forth. He was over fifty, bald, in an office, decent in mind and habits, of uncertain opinions, uncertain politics, and uncertain religion. Yet he considered himself a decided, positive gentleman, quite unaware that the morning newspaper determined his opinions for the day. He just lived—from day to day. Physically, he was fit enough, except for a weak heart (which never troubled him); and his summer holiday was bad golf, while the children bathed and his wife read Garvice on the sands. Like the majority of men, he dreamed idly of the past, muddled away the present, and guessed vaguely—after imaginative reading on occasions—at the future.

'I'd like to survive all right,' he said, 'provided it's better than this,' surveying his wife and children, and thinking of his daily toil. 'Otherwise—!' and he shrugged his shoulders as a brave man should.

He went to church regularly. But nothing in church

convinced him that he did survive, just as nothing in church enticed him into hoping that he would. On the other hand, nothing in life persuaded him that he didn't, wouldn't, couldn't. 'I'm an Evolutionist,' he loved to say to thoughtful cronies (over a glass), having never heard that Darwinism had been questioned.

And so he came home gaily, happily, with his bunch of Christmas Presents 'for the wife and little ones,' stroking himself upon their keen enjoyment and excitement. The night before he had taken 'the wife' to see *Magic* at a select London theatre where the Intellectuals went—and had been extraordinarily stirred. He had gone questioningly, yet expecting something out of the common. 'It's *not* musical,' he warned her, 'nor farce, nor comedy, so to speak', and in answer to her question as to what the critics had said, he had wriggled, sighed, and put his gaudy neck-tie straight four times in quick succession. For no Man in the Street, with any claim to self-respect, could be expected to understand what the critics had said, even if he understood the Play. And John had answered truthfully: 'Oh, they just said things. But the theatre's always full—and that's the only test.'

And just now, as he crossed the crowded Circus to catch his 'bus, it chanced that his mind (having glimpsed an advertisement) was full of this particular Play, or, rather, of the effect it had produced upon him at the time. For it had thrilled him—inexplicably: with its marvellous speculative hint, its big audacity, its alert and spiritual beauty... Thought plunged to find something—plunged after this bizarre suggestion of a bigger universe, after this quasi-jocular suggestion that man is not the only—then dashed full-tilt against a sentence that memory thrust beneath his nose: 'Science does *not* exhaust the Universe'—and at the same time dashed full-tilt against destruction of another kind as well...!

How it happened he never exactly knew. He saw a Monster glaring at him with eyes of blazing fire. It was horrible! It rushed upon him. He dodged... Another monster met him round the corner. Both came at him simultaneously. He dodged again—a leap that might have cleared a hurdle easily, but was too late. Between the pair of them—his heart literally in his gullet—he was mercilessly caught. Bones crunched... There was a soft sensation, icy cold and hot as fire. Horns and voices roared. Battering-rams he saw, and a carapace of iron... Then dazzling light... 'Always *face* the traffic!' he remembered with a frantic yell—and, by some extraordinary luck, escaped miraculously on to the opposite pavement.

There was no doubt about it. By the skin of his teeth he had dodged a rather ugly death. First... he felt for his Presents—all were safe. And then, instead of congratulating himself and taking breath, he hurried homewards—on foot, which proved that his mind had lost control a bit!—thinking only how disappointed the wife and children would have been if—well, if anything had happened. Another thing he realised, oddly enough, was that he no longer really loved his wife, but had only great affection for her. What made him think of that, Heaven only knows, but he *did* think of it. He was an honest man without pretence. This came as a discovery somehow. He turned a moment, and saw the crowd gathered about the entangled taxi-cabs, policemen's helmets gleaming in the lights of the shop windows... then hurried on again, his thoughts full of the joy his Presents would give... of the scampering children... and of his wife—bless her silly heart!—eyeing the mysterious parcels...

And, though he never could explain how, he presently stood at the door of the jail-like building that contained his flat, having walked the whole three miles. His thoughts had been so busy and absorbed that he had hardly noticed the length of weary trudge. 'Besides,' he reflected, thinking of the narrow escape, 'I've had a nasty shock. It was a damned near thing, now I come to think of it...' He still felt a bit shaky and bewildered. Yet, at the same time, he felt extraordinarily jolly and light-hearted.

He counted his Christmas parcels... hugged himself in anticipatory joy—and let himself in swiftly with his latch-key. 'I'm late,' he realised, 'but when she sees the brown-paper parcels, she'll forget to say a word. God bless the old faithful soul.' And he softly used the key a second time and entered his flat on tiptoe... In his mind was the master impulse of that afternoon—the pleasure these Christmas Presents would give his wife and children.

He heard a noise. He hung up hat and coat in the poky vestibule (they never called it 'hall') and moved softly towards the parlour door, holding the packages behind him. Only of them he thought, not of himself—of his family, that is, not of the packages. Pushing the door cunningly ajar, he peeped in shyly. To his amazement the room was full of people. He withdrew quickly, wondering what it meant. A party? And without his knowing about it? Extraordinary!... Keen disappointment came over him. But as he stepped back, the vestibule, he saw, was full of people too.

He was uncommonly surprised, yet somehow not surprised at all. People were congratulating him. There was a perfect mob of them. Moreover, he knew them all—vaguely remembered them, at least. And they all knew him.

'Isn't it a game?' laughed someone, patting him on the back. '*They* haven't the least idea…!'

And the speaker, it was old John Palmer, the bookkeeper at the office—emphasised the 'they.'

'Not the least idea,' he answered with a smile, saying something he didn't understand, yet knew was right.

His face, apparently, showed the utter bewilderment he felt. The shock of the collision had been greater than he realised evidently. His mind was wandering… Possibly! Only the odd thing was—he had never felt so clear-headed in his life. Ten thousand things grew simple suddenly. But, how thickly these people pressed about him, and how—familiarly!

'My parcels,' he said, joyously pushing his way across the throng. 'These are Christmas Presents I've bought for them.' He nodded toward the room. 'I've saved for weeks—stopped cigars and billiards and—and several other good things—to buy them.'

'Good man!' said Palmer with a happy laugh. 'It's the heart that counts.'

Mudbury looked at him. Palmer had said an amazing truth, only—people would hardly understand and believe him… Would they?

'Eh?' he asked, feeling stuffed and stupid, muddled somewhere between two meanings, one of which was gorgeous and the other stupid beyond belief.

'If you *please*, Mr. Mudbury, step inside. They are expecting you,' said a kindly, pompous voice. And, turning sharply, he met the gentle, foolish eyes of Sir James Epiphany, a director of the Bank where he worked.

The effect of the voice was instantaneous from long habit.

'They are,' he smiled from his heart, and advanced as from the custom of many years. Oh, how happy and gay he felt! His affection for his wife was real. Romance, indeed, had gone, but he needed her—and she needed him. And the children—Milly, Bill, and Jean—he deeply loved them. Life was worth living indeed!

In the room was a crowd, but—an astounding silence. John Mudbury looked round him. He advanced towards his wife, who sat in the corner armchair with Milly on her knee. A lot of people talked and moved about. Momentarily the crowd increased. He stood in front of them—in front of Milly and his wife. And he spoke—holding out his packages. 'It's Christmas Eve,' he whispered shyly, 'and I've—brought you something— something for everybody. Look!' He held the packages before their eyes.

'Of course, of course,' said a voice behind him, 'but you may hold them out like that for a century. They'll *never* see them!'

'Of course they won't. But I love to do the old, sweet thing,' replied John Mudbury—then wondered with a gasp of stark amazement why he said it.

'*I* think—' whispered Milly, staring round her.

'Well what do you think?' her mother asked sharply. 'You're always thinking something odd.'

'I think,' the girl continued dreamily, 'that Daddy's already here.' She paused, then added with a child's impossible conviction, 'I'm sure he is. I *feel* him.'

There was an extraordinary laugh. Sir James Epiphany laughed. The others—the whole crowd of them—also turned their heads and smiled. But the mother, thrusting the child away from her, rose up suddenly with a violent start. Her face had turned to chalk. She stretched her arms out into the air before her. She gasped and shivered. There was anguish in her eyes.

'Look!' repeated John, 'these are the Presents that I brought.'

But his voice apparently was soundless. And, with a spasm of icy pain, he remembered that Palmer and Sir James—some years ago—had died.

'It's magic,' he cried, 'but—I love you, Jinny—I love you—and—and I have always been true to you—as true as steel. We need each other—oh, can't you see—we go on together—you and I—for ever and ever—'

'*Think*,' interrupted an exquisitely tender voice, 'don't shout! They can't *hear* you—now.' And, turning, John Mudbury met the eyes of Everard Minturn, their President of the year before. Minturn had gone down with the *Titanic*.

He dropped his parcels then. His heart gave an enormous leap of joy.

He saw her face—the face of his wife—look through him.

But the child gazed straight into his eyes. She *saw* him.

The next thing he knew was that he heard something tinkling... far, far away. It sounded miles below him—inside him—he was sounding himself—all utterly bewildering—like a bell. It *was* a bell.

Milly stooped down and picked the parcels up. Her face shone with happiness and laughter...

But a man came in soon after, a man with a ridiculous, solemn face, a pencil and a notebook. He wore a dark blue helmet. Behind him came a string of other men. They carried something... something... he could not see exactly what it was. But, when he pressed forward through the laughing throng to gaze upon it, he dimly made out two eyes, a nose, a chin, a deep red smear, and a pair of folded hands upon an overcoat. A woman's form fell down upon them then, and he heard soft sounds of children weeping strangely... and other sounds... as of familiar voices laughing... laughing gaily.

'They'll join us presently. It goes like a flash...'

And, turning with great happiness in his heart, he saw that Sir James had said it, holding Palmer by the arm as with some natural yet unexpected love of sympathetic friendship.

'Come on,' said Palmer, smiling like a man who accepts a gift in universal fellowship, 'let's help 'em. They'll never understand... Still, we can always try.'

The entire throng moved up with laughter and amusement. It was a moment of hearty, genuine life at last. Delight and Joy and Peace were everywhere.

Then John Mudbury realised the truth—that he was dead.

THE FOURTH WALL

A. M. Burrage

FIRST PUBLISHED IN *THE LONDON MAGAZINE*, DECEMBER 1915

Alfred McLelland Burrage (1889–1956) came from a family dependent on the magazine industry. Both his father and his uncle were writers of adventure stories for periodicals aimed at boys. His father died when Alfred was still at school and he quickly began submitting his own stories to magazines, probably in an attempt to keep the family solvent. The same month this story was published, December 1915, Burrage attested under the Derby Scheme – which means that he volunteered to enlist as a soldier if called upon. He did fight in World War I, continuing to send stories home for publication, although this was awkward as mail was censored and understandably the army was not keen on having to get through sheaves of pages of fiction in addition to conventional letters. His works were mainly either romance and adventure hybrids, or ghost stories.

When Forran complained of pains in the head, a steadily declining appetite, and a growing difficulty in getting to sleep, his wife urged him to waste no more faith on the local practitioner and spend two guineas on a visit to some great man in Harley Street. And after two months of gentle bullying, and a miserable consciousness of growing worse instead of better, Forran went.

The Harley Street doctor earned his two guineas in as many minutes. When Forran left the house he found himself pledged to give up work for at least two months, and rest in some quiet and bracing part of the country. Forran was one of three partners in a firm of solicitors, and as he was not a poor man it was not difficult for him to arrange for an eight or nine weeks' holiday. His idea was to take a furnished cottage within easy distance of some pike fishing, and where rough shooting might also be obtained. Mrs. Forran was to accompany him.

At first, their plan was to go away by themselves, but it occurred to Forran that such an arrangement might be very dull for poor Betty, and Mrs. Forran thought that a little company other than her own might be good for dear Jack. Thus it came about that Tom and Helen Marriott, Mrs. Forran's brother and sister, were urged to join them.

At that time I was just beginning to realise that life without Helen would be worse than a lingering death; so I angled tactfully for an invitation, which eventually I received from Mrs. Forran, who saw how it was with me. So we went away five strong, a happy little party, whose members could be relied upon to live for two months under the same roof without wearing upon each other.

Jack Forran saw the advertisement of the furnished cottage in a weekly paper devoted to such things, and Tom went down into Huntingdonshire to look at it. He returned full of ecstasies. He had never seen such a cottage, he said; and in five minutes we had caught his enthusiasm. It was very old, and had been endowed with the comforts of civilisation without losing its antiquity. It was furnished throughout with genuine old furniture, and the whole place contained nothing shoddy and not one jarring note. In a word, it was the cottage one often dreams of but seldom sees.

For the rest, Tom had to admit that it was miles from any town or village, but he argued that this seclusion was just what we wanted. Moreover, the Great Ouse was only half an hour's walk distant, and there, he told us, the wildfowl were crying aloud to be shot and the pike begging to be caught. So Jack, without wasting time, wrote to the London agent, and took this paragon of cottages for two months, antique furniture and all.

We arrived on a December evening, having driven five miles in a slow trap from a little village station on the branch line from Cambridge. Our cottage stood just outside the region of the fens, but it had been built on the crest of what passes for a hill in that part of the country, and Tom guaranteed it to be fairly dry. In other respects we were prepared for disappointments, for we had begun to fear that he had made us expect too much. We got ready to fall upon him and find fault.

But when the door was opened to us, and one after another we crossed the threshold into a warm room flooded with soft light, we were all ready to swear that Tom had done the place less than justice.

The door opened straight into the one large living-room, and opposite to us a grandfather's clock ticked loudly and with elderly precision. On our right hand logs were burning on the wide, open hearth, in the ingles of which were chintz-covered seats. Already I fancied myself there with Helen, we two alone in the firelight, watching the grey smoke curling up into the wide chimney. Heavy beams supported the low ceiling, and one ran diagonally along the cream-washed wall, sloping downwards from the ceiling and disappearing behind the clock.

Beside the clock were two doors, one leading to the kitchen and the other to the stairs. There was another door on our left as we entered, and that led into a small apartment fitted up as a morning-room or study. These details are important in view of what follows.

Supper was ready, but we explored the rest of the cottage before sitting down to it. I don't think we met with one disappointment. There was even a bathroom. 'So,' Tom said to me triumphantly, 'you won't have to sponge yourself over, standing up on one leg in a kind of degraded frying pan.'

Mrs. Forran had arranged for a woman to come in every morning and do the rough work, since there was no room there for a servant to sleep. The woman was present when we arrived, and had prepared a hot meal for us. Her younger sister had come, too, to keep her company.

This Mrs. Lubbock was a stumpy, silent creature, seemingly very nervous and stupid, and it was hard to get more than a word out of her. She did not know to whom the cottage belonged, or so she said. A gentleman named Sellinger used to come and stop there, but him she had hardly seen, and knew nothing about. She looked nervously around her as she said this, and left as soon as we would let her, dragging her sister with her.

In the interval between her departure and our sitting down to the roast ham and fowls, Tom nodded to me to come into the kitchen. I did so, and he pointed to the inside of the door, on which a cross had been roughly drawn with a piece of white chalk. I looked at him and saw him smiling, his eyebrows lifted.

'That's that woman,' he remarked. 'Do you know what it means, Archie?'

'I suppose it means that she thinks the house is haunted,' I said, 'I should think the people round here are pretty superstitious. They generally are in these lonely places.'

Tom sank his voice.

'Don't say anything to Jack,' he whispered.

'Pooh! Jack doesn't believe in spooks. He's not such a fool.'

'Nevertheless, he's not himself these days, and we won't take any risks. Look out!'

He took out his handkerchief and smudged the chalk marks until the cross was obliterated. 'By Jove,' he added, 'this is "some" cottage! Ghost and all!'

'We ought to have a sweepstake,' I suggested. 'The money to go to the first who sees it.'

'Could we trust each other, do you think?' said Tom, and we both laughed.

It would be well to explain at once that none of us believed in what is commonly called the supernatural. We were normal, hard-headed people, even more sceptical concerning such things as ghosts than the average man in the street. At ordinary times we should have welcomed a ghost story connected with our dwelling-place, but, as Tom had said, Jack Forran was not quite himself.

During supper we criticised the cottage, and Jack was the only one who had something to say about it that fell short of praise.

'It's a ripping old place,' he said; 'but do you know it seems to me rather self-conscious of being a cottage.'

'What do you mean?' Mrs. Forran laughed.

'I mean that everything about it—the furniture and all that— is so very "cottagey". It seems to keep on shouting at you: "I am a cottage. Everything in me is just right for a cottage." I don't express myself very well.'

Helen laughed.

'I know,' she said. 'You mean this room is, somehow, just a little stagey.'

'Stagey was just the very word I was trying to think of,' Jack said. Tom, who was sitting opposite Helen and me, looked around him. 'Do you know,' he said, 'that this room is just like a scene on the stage. Try and imagine that wall over there—the fourth wall I think it's called—has been taken down. On the floor is a row of footlights. Beyond it's all dark, and there is row after row of blurred faces.'

Mrs. Forran nodded, and we all looked round at the fourth wall. 'Yes, I can imagine all that,' she said.

'Well, then,' Tom continued, 'imagine yourself among the audience for a moment. You'd be looking on to the stage at a

conventional stage cottage sitting-room. That door leading to
the little room would be the exit on the prompt side. There's no
exit on the other side, but the space behind the chimney looks
like one. Open hearth on right. Two doors at back, grandfather's
clock, oak beams, everything complete.'

We all marvelled, because it was in very truth a perfect
stage cottage, and I immediately experienced what I took to be
the power of suggestion. I was sitting beside Helen, with my
back to the fourth wall, and I felt that there was no wall there.
Behind me was a row of bright footlights, and a sea of dim faces.
I could feel hundreds of eyes upon me, and even suffered for
the moment a mild kind of stage fright.

Now I am not one given to nerves, nor is my imagination in
the ordinary way a particularly active one. But on that occasion
it seemed to slip out of my control, and I imagined not only that
the fourth wall was down, but that all our little party began to
behave in a certain precise and self-conscious manner as if they
were acting before an audience. And I, too, although I strove
against it, became one of the mummers.

When we spoke we pitched our voices in a slightly higher
key, and made our articulation clearer. We addressed each other
not in our usual manner, but as rather stiff strangers who had
been placed at the same table at an hotel. Our table manners lost
their freedom. Jack, who was inclined to sprawl in his chair, sat
up straight as a ramrod. Tom, who had a habit of playing with
his breadcrumbs while he was not actually eating, sat between
the courses with his hands under the table. The idea that the
wall was down and the audience watching our every movement
and listening to every word seemed to have worked ridiculously
on the minds of us all.

We were talking primly in our stupid stage voices about something quite unimportant, when Tom, who had been silent for a while, suddenly startled us. He raised his voice, and, looking over the heads of Helen and me, declaimed as follows:

'When I do fall in love, Heaven help me—and her!'

The voice was hardly his own; it was the sonorous, flexible voice of an actor. The words boomed from his lips, full of passion and sadness. I felt Helen start beside me. We had not been talking of love, and in the circumstances I had never heard a less pertinent speech. There was dead silence for nearly half a minute.

Then I felt a change come over me, as if a shadow had passed on from my mind. I felt no more the footlights behind me and the rows of faces, and suddenly set up a roar of laughter. Simultaneously all the others laughed.

Once again we were old friends, supping privately and behaving naturally, no longer mummers on a stage. We laughed until the tears ran down our cheeks.

'Oh, Tom, you idiot!' Helen cried.

'What on earth made you say that?' Mrs. Forran demanded, choking.

Tom regarded us all, smiling but slightly flushed.

'I don't know,' he said. 'It must have sounded frightfully mad. The words came into my head, and I just said them.'

Afterwards they became a catch-phrase with us. Now we all repeated them, imitating Tom's voice, until Mrs. Forran sniffed audibly, and looked towards the fire.

'Can you smell anything burning?' she asked.

We all could. There was a heavy smell of smoke in the air. It was as if a part of the carpet were smouldering.

'A spark must have jumped out of the fire,' I said; and went to see. But I could find nothing, although I searched the room, and presently the smell of burning went. We agreed that it was rather curious.

We had been at the cottage more than a week when, just after tea on a dark, drizzling evening, Tom begged me to come out for a walk with him. It was not inviting outside, and I was never glad to leave Helen, but the look in her brother's eyes made me aware that he had something to say to me. So I assented rather grudgingly, and put on my cap and Ulster.

Up to then we had had a good time. I was always happy when I was near Helen; Jack was already much better, and everybody was delighted at the signs he displayed of an early recovery. Moreover, we had had plenty of sport with our guns, and Jack had landed an eleven-pound pike on a spinner.

All that marred our pleasure was that sensation of being on the stage, to which all of us had to confess. Generally it came on at supper, and then we made frantic efforts to behave like our normal selves. Fifty times a day we bullied Tom for giving voice to the suggestion, and thus affecting all of us.

There was also a mystery, which we had given up trying to solve. Regularly every evening at about the same time we smelt something burning, and always we searched for a smouldering splinter on the carpet, and never found it. Jack had a theory beginning, 'When the wind is in a certain quarter...' which we accepted, but only because a poor explanation is better than none to people who do not care for being mystified.

As Tom and I picked our way down the dark garden, sucking at our pipes, I knew instinctively that he wanted to talk to me about the cottage. For some reason I did not care to be too serious, and as we reached the road I imitated his voice, saying:

'When I do fall in love, Heaven help me—and her!' He laughed, but not very mirthfully.

'Yes,' he said, 'that was dashed queer. Archie, my dear lad, there are a lot of things that are very queer. Have you any vices?'

'Such as?'

'Going downstairs at night and reading your immortal short stories aloud to yourself?'

'Me!' I exclaimed. 'Good Lord, no! Why?'

'Well, Jack had a jolly good night's sleep last night, so it wasn't he. It certainly wasn't I. And now you say it wasn't you. And it was a man's voice.'

I felt an uncomfortable, prickly feeling in my skin. 'What are you talking about?' I asked.

He hesitated a moment.

'Look here,' he said, 'Helen's had a fright. You know her room is over the dining-room? Well, it seems she woke up last night quite late, and heard a man's voice in the room underneath. It sounded quite plain—so plain that she could almost hear the words. It was like somebody reading aloud with a lot of expression. She didn't know the voice.'

Again I felt that prickly sensation in my skin. 'She must have been dreaming,' I said.

'My dear chap, a week ago I should have declared unhesitatingly that she was dreaming. But now I'm not so sure.'

'You say it was like somebody reading aloud?'

'Yes, with a lot of expression. An actor going through his part, for instance.'

93

He said this with an elaborate casualness, but I caught another note in his voice. 'Tom,' I said, 'don't be an idiot.'

He was silent for a short while. Presently he said:

'You don't believe in ghosts, of course?'

'No, I don't.'

'Nor did I until the last few days. It's no use howling me down, Archie, but there is something queer about that cottage. For instance, that sensation of being on the stage before an audience. We all get it at times. And the smell of burning. And the queer thing I said almost unconsciously that you all rag me about.'

I was already more than half convinced, but I tried to argue on the side of what I thought was sanity.

'Are you sure we haven't all caught nerves from poor old Jack?' I suggested.

'Nerves! Rubbish! Besides, old Jack is, luckily, the least affected by these things of all of us. That's because he doesn't believe in uncanny things, and he doesn't know all that we know. Helen told nobody but me about the man she heard reading, simply because she wanted it kept from Jack. And he doesn't know about the cross we found on the kitchen door. If anything happens to give him a bad shock—well, you know what the result might be. I think we ought to try to get him away.'

Still I argued.

'The cross we found on the kitchen door proves that the silly old charwoman thought the cottage was haunted. And you know what country people are.'

Tom looked at me queerly.

'Look here, old chap,' he said, 'when we came here we didn't believe in such things. We all rather prided ourselves on being hard-headed. But now don't you think, after what has happened, that we might as well revise our views a little? Even if we would like to believe otherwise, don't for Heaven's sake let us shut our eyes to proofs. Supernatural or not, there is something confoundedly queer about the place we're living in. If Jack gets a bad shock it may send him mad. And poor Helen's frightened.'

Those two arguments were enough to make me see that we ought to leave the cottage. But the problem of how to get Jack to go was not easily solved. He was so thoroughly in love with his surroundings that no trivial objection would dislodge him, while to tell him the truth would simply defeat our own ends.

We talked this over for some time, but found no way out of the difficulty.

Then Helen began to occupy all my thoughts, and I insisted on our going back. She was safe enough with Jack and Mrs. Forran, but I felt somehow that my place was near her. And Tom grabbed me by the shoulder with his long fingers, and let me know by a peculiar chuckle that he understood.

The evening of the twenty-second of December will live long in my memory, and with good reason. Let me try to tell what happened plainly and straightforwardly, without the omission of any important detail, and yet without exaggeration.

We had then occupied the cottage for about a fortnight, and since my walk in the rain with Tom—when he had confessed his sudden belief in 'ghosts'—nothing of importance had happened. We had experienced as usual the smell of burning, and the queer sensation of being on the stage, but Helen had heard no more voices, nor had there been any fresh phenomena.

After tea on that particular evening it was arranged that we should drive into St. Ives and do some shopping; but I, seeing a Heaven-sent opportunity to do some of the work which I had neglected of late, elected to stay behind. I will not pretend that I was not nervous, but I will stoutly maintain, until the last day I live, that my nerves played no part in deluding me.

At first, when I was left alone and sat down to write, I felt 'jumpy' and uncomfortable. But a couple of pipes soothed me, and I soon lost myself in my work. After a while my pen began to scrape, paused, and went on scraping in the old familiar way. The old grandfather's clock said 'tock-tock, tock-tock', until I got so used to his voice that it seemed to become part of the silence.

Work passes the time as quickly as play, and when I paused to light another pipe and looked up at the clock, I found, to my surprise, that more than two hours had slipped away. It would not be very long before the others returned, so I went on with my work at once, and became absorbed in it for another half-hour.

Then quite suddenly I felt grow upon me that feeling of self-consciousness that I was beginning to know so well. I felt that hundreds of eyes were upon me, that hundreds of people were waiting to see what I would do next, and hear what I would say. I felt the cold air of fear in my nostrils, a dreadful sinking in the stomach, a prickly feeling in the skin.

'Nerves!' I told myself; but I dared not raise my eyes. I sat still, with my gaze bent down upon the uncompleted sentence, my pen shaking in my fingers. The grandfather's clock ticked on slowly, and I sat quite still, the slave of fear.

At last, and never so slowly and stealthily, I raised my eyes. They rested upon the door leading into the morning-room, which stood ajar. It was dark inside, but certain things were dimly visible, and those things were unfamiliar.

I saw the half of a step-ladder, the corner of what looked like a rough wooden shed, and a piece of rope dangling. My heart gave a great leap, and then seemed to stop beating.

'Oh, my God!' was the thought that leaped into my brain. 'The wings of a theatre!'

I moved my gaze round a little to the left, and instead of seeing the wall—the fourth wall—I saw a space of semi-gloom. Beyond the carpet was a short space of bare boards, and then a row of footlights throwing up a yellow glare. In the gloom I saw faces, row upon row of them, the curves of a dress circle and gallery with a glint of light on their brass railings, and high up in a kind of dome a cluster of small lamps was burning dimly.

I sprang up with a little cry, and stood facing the ghastly change that had overtaken the wall. There was not a sound, but I was horribly conscious of the undivided attention of hundreds upon hundreds of eyes and ears. And as I stood, dumb and quaking, my nostrils caught an acrid whiff of smoke.

Simultaneously I heard a sharp scream behind me. A hoarse voice shouted something inaudible. Heavy footfalls began to ring on hollow boarding; I heard a hiss like an escape of steam, and the clatter of pails.

Then I spoke, and the voice sounded in no way like my own. I said: 'If I do fall in love, Heaven help me—and her!'

I uttered the words without realising their meaning, and because I was powerless to do otherwise.

Then the faces of that ghastly audience dimmed, and finally vanished, cut off from me by a curtain of black smoke. The smoke was all around me in reeking clouds. It got into my eyes and my throat, and I fell forward, choking and gasping, on to my knees. An agony of suffocation tore me. As consciousness slipped away from me I have a dim memory of a great tongue of flame flickering a yard in front of my eyes...

It was Helen who found me lying on the floor. She had run in a little in advance of the others, and the sight of me, lying thus, gave her the greatest fright of her experience. What she said to me before I came round I never learned until we became engaged, and that is neither here nor there. After a minute the others came in, and I have a dim memory of being given brandy and led up to bed.

Next day I lied painfully to my fellow members of the household, assuring them that I was only the victim of a heart attack, the first of my experience. But later in the morning Tom came and sat on the edge of my bed, fixing me with a pair of quizzical eyes.

'Better now?' he asked.

'Much.'

'Then you can tell me what happened. Heart attack be hanged. I've already prepared Jack for what I'm going to tell him. We're going to clear out of this at once. Will you tell your story first, or shall I tell mine?'

I looked at him in surprise.

'Has anything fresh happened?'

'I found out something yesterday,' he answered. 'The cottage is supposed to be haunted, although nobody seems to know precisely in what way. But I've found out all about the man who used to live here, and it seems to fit in rather well with what we've all experienced. Shall I tell you?'

'Yes, do!'

'Well, then. Yesterday evening, while the others were buying groceries, I went in to an inn at St. Ives to get a bottle of whisky. There was a farmer chap in the bar, and I started talking to him, and told him where we were stopping. He pricked up his ears at once, and asked if we'd seen the ghost. I told him no, and asked him about it. He said that the cottage was supposed to be haunted by a man named Sellinger, who had lived in it off and on for years.'

'An actor?'

'Yes, an actor. It seems he used to use the place always when he was resting. He was quite a celebrity in his way, although he was hardly known to the London stage. For years he'd been touring the provinces with a play called *The Heart of Annette*, in which he played the lead. There was a scene in the play which depicted the interior of an old cottage, and from that scene he copied the arrangement of the room downstairs in every detail.'

'Ah!' I said, and shuddered. Already I had a dim idea of what was coming.

'He loved this place,' Tom resumed, 'and every weekend he could spare he came down here. All his vacations, too, were spent here. You can imagine him going through his parts in that room downstairs.'

I nodded grimly. My imagination needed very little stimulation.

'About a year ago,' Tom continued, 'he met his death on the stage. He was playing at a theatre in the Midlands, and was in the middle of his scene in the cottage sitting-room when the stage caught fire. He was suffocated by the smoke. He had just said, "If I fall in love, Heaven help me—and her!" when the smoke and flame rushed in upon him. Those were his last words. Why, what's the matter, Archie?'

There is a theory that when a man loves the place he lives in, it remains imbued with his personality long after he has left it. There is another theory to the effect that the spirit of a very strong personality (such as the actor Sellinger had doubtless been) can impress upon the minds of living people mental pictures of places and incidents which have figured prominently in his life, and can even make them experience the sense of a certain smell—as of burning, for instance. The spirit could, indeed, on rare occasions actually 'control' a person still in the flesh, and make him utter words quite involuntarily. As to that, let each think as he will.

But we were practical people, and we did not theorise overmuch. We simply left the cottage and went to Malvern. Anybody may have that cottage at a very modest rental, but we do not recommend it. There may not be such things as ghosts, but there are a lot of things, pleasant and unpleasant, which are beyond our ken.

THE FESTIVAL

H. P. Lovecraft

FIRST PUBLISHED IN *WEIRD TALES*, JANUARY 1925

Howard Phillips Lovecraft (1890–1937) was born in Providence, Rhode Island, and lived most of his life in New England. When his father died of syphilis in 1898, he and his mother moved into her parental home. Lovecraft's interest in literature came from his maternal grandfather, who invented 'weird tales' for him. Lovecraft struggled with depression and other mental health issues throughout his life. His career as an author began as a result of writing critical letters to early pulp magazines, and he later started to submit stories of his own. At the time this story was published, he was living in a single room apartment in Brooklyn, New York, in poverty, and that same year was working on the outline for *The Call of Cthulhu*, a novelette which would later become one of his most influential works. Despite being regularly published in the magazine *Weird Tales* and elsewhere, he was not well known in his lifetime and struggled financially until his death at the age of 46 from cancer of the small intestine.

Today, whilst few would deny Lovecraft's huge importance as an influence on later horror, science fiction and fantasy writers, his legacy is tarnished by the racist, homophobic and misogynistic beliefs he held.

'Efficiunt Daemones, ut quae non sunt, sic tamen quasi sint, conspicienda hominibus exhibeant.'

—*Lactantius.*

I was far from home, and the spell of the eastern sea was upon me. In the twilight I heard it pounding on the rocks, and I knew it lay just over the hill where the twisting willows writhed against the clearing sky and the first stars of evening. And because my fathers had called me to the old town beyond, I pushed on through the shallow, new-fallen snow along the road that soared lonely up to where Aldebaran twinkled among the trees; on toward the very ancient town I had never seen but often dreamed of.

It was the Yuletide, that men call Christmas though they know in their hearts it is older than Bethlehem and Babylon, older than Memphis and mankind. It was the Yuletide, and I had come at last to the ancient sea town where my people had dwelt and kept festival in the elder time when festival was forbidden; where also they had commanded their sons to keep festival once every century, that the memory of primal secrets might not be forgotten. Mine were an old people, and were old even when this land was settled three hundred years before. And they were strange, because they had come as dark furtive folk from opiate southern gardens of orchids, and spoken another tongue before they learnt the tongue of the blue-eyed fishers. And now they were scattered, and shared only the rituals of mysteries that none living could understand. I was the only one who came back that night to the old fishing town as legend bade, for only the poor and the lonely remember.

Then beyond the hill's crest I saw Kingsport outspread frostily in the gloaming; snowy Kingsport with its ancient vanes and steeples, ridgepoles and chimney-pots, wharves and small bridges, willow-trees and graveyards; endless labyrinths of steep, narrow, crooked streets, and dizzy church-crowned central peak that time durst not touch; ceaseless mazes of colonial houses piled and scattered at all angles and levels like a child's disordered blocks; antiquity hovering on grey wings over winter-whitened gables and gambrel roofs; fanlights and small-paned windows one by one gleaming out in the cold dusk to join Orion and the archaic stars. And against the rotting wharves the sea pounded; the secretive, immemorial sea out of which the people had come in the elder time.

Beside the road at its crest a still higher summit rose, bleak and windswept, and I saw that it was a burying-ground where black gravestones stuck ghoulishly through the snow like the decayed fingernails of a gigantic corpse. The printless road was very lonely, and sometimes I thought I heard a distant horrible creaking as of a gibbet in the wind. They had hanged four kinsmen of mine for witchcraft in 1692, but I did not know just where.

As the road wound down the seaward slope I listened for the merry sounds of a village at evening, but did not hear them. Then I thought of the season, and felt that these old Puritan folk might well have Christmas customs strange to me, and full of silent hearthside prayer. So after that I did not listen for merriment or look for wayfarers, but kept on down past the hushed lighted farmhouses and shadowy stone walls to where the signs of ancient shops and sea-taverns creaked in the salt breeze, and the grotesque knockers of pillared doorways glistened along deserted, unpaved lanes in the light of little, curtained windows.

I had seen maps of the town, and knew where to find the home of my people. It was told that I should be known and welcomed, for village legend lives long; so I hastened through Back Street to Circle Court, and across the fresh snow on the one full flagstone pavement in the town, to where Green Lane leads off behind the Market House. The old maps still held good, and I had no trouble; though at Arkham they must have lied when they said the trolleys ran to this place, since I saw not a wire overhead. Snow would have hid the rails in any case. I was glad I had chosen to walk, for the white village had seemed very beautiful from the hill; and now I was eager to knock at the door of my people, the seventh house on the left in Green Lane, with an ancient peaked roof and jutting second storey, all built before 1650.

There were lights inside the house when I came upon it, and I saw from the diamond window-panes that it must have been kept very close to its antique state. The upper part overhung the narrow grass-grown street and nearly met the overhanging part of the house opposite, so that I was almost in a tunnel, with the low stone doorstep wholly free from snow. There was no sidewalk, but many houses had high doors reached by double flights of steps with iron railings. It was an odd scene, and because I was strange to New England I had never known its like before. Though it pleased me, I would have relished it better if there had been footprints in the snow, and people in the streets, and a few windows without drawn curtains.

When I sounded the archaic iron knocker I was half afraid. Some fear had been gathering in me, perhaps because of the strangeness of my heritage, and the bleakness of the evening, and the queerness of the silence in that aged town of curious customs. And when my knock was answered I was fully afraid, because I had not heard any footsteps before the door creaked open. But I was not afraid long, for the gowned, slippered old man in the doorway had a bland face that reassured me; and though he made signs that he was dumb, he wrote a quaint and ancient welcome with the stylus and wax tablet he carried.

He beckoned me into a low, candle-lit room with massive exposed rafters and dark, stiff, sparse furniture of the seventeenth century. The past was vivid there, for not an attribute was missing. There was a cavernous fireplace and a spinning-wheel at which a bent old woman in loose wrapper and deep poke-bonnet sat back toward me, silently spinning despite the festive season. An indefinite dampness seemed upon the place, and I marvelled that no fire should be blazing. The high-backed settle faced the row of curtained windows at the left, and seemed to be occupied, though I was not sure. I did not like everything about what I saw, and felt again the fear I had had. This fear grew stronger from what had before lessened it, for the more I looked at the old man's bland face the more its very blandness terrified me. The eyes never moved, and the skin was too like wax. Finally I was sure it was not a face at all, but a fiendishly cunning mask. But the flabby hands, curiously gloved, wrote genially on the tablet and told me I must wait a while before I could be led to the place of the festival.

Pointing to a chair, table, and pile of books, the old man now left the room; and when I sat down to read I saw that the books were hoary and mouldy, and that they included old Morryster's wild 'Marvells of Science', the terrible 'Saducismus Triumphatus' of Joseph Glanvill, published in 1681, the shocking 'Daemonolatreia' of Remigius, printed in 1595 at Lyons, and worst of all, the unmentionable 'Necronomicon' of the mad Arab Abdul Alhazred, in Olaus Wormius' forbidden Latin translation; a book which I had never seen, but of which I had heard monstrous things whispered. No one spoke to me, but I could hear the creaking of signs in the wind outside, and the whir of the wheel as the bonneted old woman continued her silent spinning, spinning. I thought the room and the books and the people very morbid and disquieting, but because an old tradition of my fathers had summoned me to strange feastings, I resolved to expect queer things. So I tried to read, and soon became tremblingly absorbed by something I found in that accursed 'Necronomicon'; a thought and a legend too hideous for sanity or consciousness. But I disliked it when I fancied I heard the closing of one of the windows that the settle faced, as if it had been stealthily opened. It had seemed to follow a whirring that was not of the old woman's spinning-wheel. This was not much, though, for the old woman was spinning very hard, and the aged clock had been striking. After that I lost the feeling that there were persons on the settle, and was reading intently and shudderingly when the old man came back booted and dressed in a loose antique costume, and sat down on that very bench, so that I could not see him. It was certainly nervous waiting, and the blasphemous book in my hands made it doubly so. When eleven struck, however, the old man stood up, glided to a massive carved chest in a corner, and got two hooded cloaks; one of which he donned, and the other of which he draped round the old woman, who was ceasing her monotonous spinning. Then they both started for the outer door; the woman lamely creeping, and the old man, after picking up the very book I had been reading, beckoning me as he drew his hood over that unmoving face or mask.

We went out into the moonless and tortuous network of that incredibly ancient town; went out as the lights in the curtained windows disappeared one by one, and the Dog Star leered at the throng of cowled, cloaked figures that poured silently from every doorway and formed monstrous processions up this street and that, past the creaking signs and antediluvian gables, the thatched roofs and diamond-paned windows; threading precipitous lanes where decaying houses overlapped and crumbled together, gliding across open courts and churchyards where the bobbing lanthorns made eldritch drunken constellations.

Amid these hushed throngs I followed my voiceless guides; jostled by elbows that seemed preternaturally soft, and pressed by chests and stomachs that seemed abnormally pulpy; but seeing never a face and hearing never a word. Up, up, up the eery columns slithered, and I saw that all the travellers were converging as they flowed near a sort of focus of crazy alleys at the top of a high hill in the centre of the town, where perched a great white church. I had seen it from the road's crest when I looked at Kingsport in the new dusk, and it had made me shiver because Aldebaran had seemed to balance itself a moment on the ghostly spire.

There was an open space around the church; partly a church-yard with spectral shafts, and partly a half-paved square swept nearly bare of snow by the wind, and lined with unwholesomely archaic houses having peaked roofs and overhanging gables. Death-fires danced over the tombs, revealing gruesome vistas, though queerly failing to cast any shadows. Past the churchyard, where there were no houses, I could see over the hill's summit and watch the glimmer of stars on the harbour, though the town was invisible in the dark. Only once in a while a lanthorn bobbed horribly through serpentine alleys on its way to overtake the throng that was now slipping speechlessly into the church. I waited till the crowd had oozed into the black doorway, and till all the stragglers had followed. The old man was pulling at my sleeve, but I was determined to be the last. Then finally I went, the sinister man and the old spinning woman before me. Crossing the threshold into that swarming temple of unknown darkness, I turned once to look at the outside world as the churchyard phosphorescence cast a sickly glow on the hilltop pavement. And as I did so I shuddered. For though the wind had not left much snow, a few patches did remain on the path near the door; and in that fleeting backward look it seemed to my troubled eyes that they bore no mark of passing feet, not even mine.

The church was scarce lighted by all the lanthorns that had entered it, for most of the throng had already vanished. They had streamed up the aisle between the high white pews to the trap-door of the vaults which yawned loathsomely open just before the pulpit, and were now squirming noiselessly in. I followed dumbly down the footworn steps and into the dank, suffocating crypt. The tail of that sinuous line of night-marchers seemed very horrible, and as I saw them wriggling into a venerable tomb they seemed more horrible still. Then I noticed that the tomb's floor had an aperture down which the throng was sliding, and in a moment we were all descending an ominous staircase of rough-hewn stone; a narrow spiral staircase damp and peculiarly odorous, that wound endlessly down into the bowels of the hill past monotonous walls of dripping stone blocks and crumbling mortar. It was a silent, shocking descent, and I observed after a horrible interval that the walls and steps were changing in nature, as if chiselled out of the solid rock. What mainly troubled me was that the myriad footfalls made no sound and set up no echoes. After more aeons of descent I saw some side passages or burrows leading from unknown recesses of blackness to this shaft of nighted mystery. Soon they became excessively numerous, like impious catacombs of nameless menace; and their pungent odour of decay grew quite unbearable. I knew we must have passed down through the mountain and beneath the earth of Kingsport itself, and I shivered that a town should be so aged and maggoty with subterraneous evil.

Then I saw the lurid shimmering of pale light, and heard the insidious lapping of sunless waters. Again I shivered, for I did not like the things that the night had brought, and wished bitterly that no forefather had summoned me to this primal rite. As the steps and the passage grew broader, I heard another sound, the thin, whining mockery of a feeble flute; and suddenly there spread out before me the boundless vista of an inner world—a vast fungous shore litten by a belching column of sick greenish flame and washed by a wide oily river that flowed from abysses frightful and unsuspected to join the blackest gulfs of immemorial ocean.

Fainting and gasping, I looked at that unhallowed Erebus of titan toadstools, leprous fire, and slimy water, and saw the cloaked throngs forming a semicircle around the blazing pillar. It was the Yule-rite, older than man and fated to survive him; the primal rite of the solstice and of spring's promise beyond the snows; the rite of fire and evergreen, light and music. And in that Stygian grotto I saw them do the rite, and adore the sick pillar of flame, and throw into the water handfuls gouged out of the viscous vegetation which glittered green in the chlorotic glare. I saw this, and I saw something amorphously squatted far away from the light, piping noisomely on a flute; and as the thing piped I thought I heard noxious muffled flutterings in the foetid darkness where I could not see. But what frightened me most was that flaming column; spouting volcanically from depths profound and inconceivable, casting no shadows as healthy flame should, and coating the nitrous stone above with a nasty, venomous verdigris. For in all that seething combustion no warmth lay, but only the clamminess of death and corruption.

The man who had brought me now squirmed to a point directly beside the hideous flame, and made stiff ceremonial motions to the semicircle he faced. At certain stages of the ritual they did grovelling obeisance, especially when he held above his head that abhorrent 'Necronomicon' he had taken with him; and I shared all the obeisances because I had been summoned to this festival by the writings of my forefathers. Then the old man made a signal to the half-seen flute-player in the darkness, which player thereupon changed its feeble drone to a scarce louder drone in another key; precipitating as it did so a horror unthinkable and unexpected. At this horror I sank nearly to the lichened earth, transfixed with a dread not of this nor any world, but only of the mad spaces between the stars.

Out of the unimaginable blackness beyond the gangrenous glare of that cold flame, out of the tartarean leagues through which that oily river rolled uncanny, unheard, and unsuspected, there flopped rhythmically a horde of tame, trained, hybrid winged things that no sound eye could ever wholly grasp, or sound brain ever wholly remember. They were not altogether crows, nor moles, nor buzzards, nor ants, nor vampire bats, nor decomposed human beings; but something I cannot and must not recall. They flopped limply along, half with their webbed feet and half with their membraneous wings; and as they reached the throng of celebrants the cowled figures seized and mounted them, and rode off one by one along the reaches of that unlighted river, into pits and galleries of panic where poison springs feed frightful and undiscoverable cataracts.

The old spinning woman had gone with the throng, and the old man remained only because I had refused when he motioned me to seize an animal and ride like the rest. I saw when I staggered to my feet that the amorphous flute-player had rolled out of sight, but that two of the beasts were patiently standing by. As I hung back, the old man produced his stylus and tablet and wrote that he was the true deputy of my fathers who had founded the Yule worship in this ancient place; that it had been decreed I should come back, and that the most secret mysteries were yet to be performed. He wrote this in a very ancient hand, and when I still hesitated he pulled from his loose robe a seal ring and a watch, both with my family arms, to prove that he was what he said. But it was a hideous proof, because

I knew from old papers that that watch had been buried with my great-great-great-great-grandfather in 1698.

Presently the old man drew back his hood and pointed to the family resemblance in his face, but I only shuddered, because I was sure that the face was merely a devilish waxen mask. The flopping animals were now scratching restlessly at the lichens, and I saw that the old man was nearly as restless himself. When one of the things began to waddle and edge away, he turned quickly to stop it; so that the suddenness of his motion dislodged the waxen mask from what should have been his head. And then, because that nightmare's position barred me from the stone staircase down which we had come, I flung myself into the oily underground river that bubbled somewhere to the caves of the sea; flung myself into that putrescent juice of earth's inner horrors before the madness of my screams could bring down upon me all the charnel legions these pest-gulfs might conceal.

At the hospital they told me I had been found half-frozen in Kingsport Harbour at dawn, clinging to the drifting spar that accident sent to save me. They told me I had taken the wrong fork of the hill road the night before, and fallen over the cliffs at Orange Point; a thing they deduced from prints found in the snow. There was nothing I could say, because everything was wrong. Everything was wrong, with the broad window shewing a sea of roofs in which only about one in five was ancient, and the sound of trolleys and motors in the streets below. They insisted that this was Kingsport, and I could not deny it. When I went delirious at hearing that the hospital stood near the old churchyard on Central Hill, they sent me to St. Mary's Hospital in Arkham, where I could have better care. I liked it there, for the doctors were broad-minded, and even lent me their influence in obtaining the carefully sheltered copy of Alhazred's objectionable 'Necronomicon' from the library of Miskatonic University. They said something about a 'psychosis', and agreed I had better get any harassing obsessions off my mind.

So I read again that hideous chapter, and shuddered doubly because it was indeed not new to me. I had seen it before, let footprints tell what they might; and where it was I had seen it were best forgotten. There was no one—in waking hours—who could remind me of it; but my dreams are filled with terror, because of phrases I dare not quote. I dare quote only one paragraph, put into such English as I can make from the awkward Low Latin.

'The nethermost caverns,' wrote the mad Arab, 'are not for the fathoming of eyes that see; for their marvels are strange and terrific. Cursed the ground where dead thoughts live new and oddly bodied, and evil the mind that is held by no head. Wisely did Ibn Schacabao say, that happy is the tomb where no wizard hath lain, and happy the town at night whose wizards are all ashes. For it is of old rumour that the soul of the devil-bought hastes not from his charnel clay, but fats and instructs *the very worm that gnaws;* till out of corruption horrid life springs, and the dull scavengers of earth wax crafty to vex it and swell monstrous to plague it. Great holes secretly are digged where earth's pores ought to suffice, and things have learnt to walk that ought to crawl.'

THE CROWN DERBY PLATE

Marjorie Bowen

PUBLISHED IN *THE LAST BOUQUET:*
SOME TWILIGHT TALES (1933)

Margaret Gabrielle Vere Campbell Long (1885–1952) had a tragic life. Her parents separated when she was a small child and she lived with her mother in poverty. She had artistic talent but various attempts to attend art college went badly due to her lack of money, and she turned to writing. Her first novel, *The Viper of Milan*, was published in 1906 – it was a success and Graham Greene later credited it with inspiring him to become an author. She was married twice, her first husband dying of tuberculosis after less than four years of marriage, and her first baby died of meningitis. She wrote under several pseudonyms – Marjorie Bowen, George Preedy, John Winch, Robert Paye and Joseph Shearing – and wrote historical romances, children's books, gothic stories and crime dramas. Her success as a novelist eventually gave her the financial stability she had lacked in her early life. This story was published in her second collection of short fiction, *The Last Bouquet: Some Twilight Tales*.

Martha Pym said that she had never seen a ghost and that she would very much like to do so, 'particularly at Christmas for you can laugh as you like, that is the correct time to see a ghost.'

'I don't suppose you ever will,' replied her cousin Mabel comfortably, while her cousin Clara shuddered and said that she hoped they would change the subject for she disliked even to think of such things.

The three elderly, cheerful women sat round a big fire, cosy and content after a day of pleasant activities; Martha was the guest of the other two, who owned the handsome, convenient country house; she always came to spend her Christmas with the Wyntons and found the leisurely country life delightful after the bustling round of London, for Martha managed an antique shop of the better sort and worked extremely hard. She was, however, still full of zest for work or pleasure, though sixty years old, and looked backwards and forwards to a succession of delightful days.

The other two, Mabel and Clara, led quieter but none the less agreeable lives; they had more money and fewer interests, but nevertheless enjoyed themselves very well.

'Talking of ghosts,' said Mabel, 'I wonder how that old woman at Hartleys is getting on, for Hartleys, you know, is supposed to be haunted.'

'Yes, I know,' smiled Miss Pym, 'but all the years that we have known of the place we have never heard anything definite, have we?'

'No,' put in Clara; 'but there *is* that persistent rumour that the house is uncanny, and for myself, *nothing* would induce me to live there!'

'It is certainly very lonely and dreary down there on the marshes,' conceded Mabel. 'But as for the ghost—you never hear *what* it is supposed to be even.'

'Who has taken it?' asked Miss Pym, remembering Hartleys as very desolate indeed, and long shut up.

'A Miss Lefain, an eccentric old creature—I think you met her here once, two years ago—'

'I believe that I did, but I don't recall her at all.'

'We have not seen her since, Hartleys is so un-get-at-able and she didn't seem to want visitors. She collects china, Martha, so really you ought to go and see her and talk "shop."'

With the word 'china' some curious associations came into the mind of Martha Pym; she was silent while she strove to put them together, and after a second or two they all fitted together into a very clear picture.

She remembered that thirty years ago—yes, it must be thirty years ago, when, as a young woman, she had put all her capital into the antique business, and had been staying with her cousins (her aunt had then been alive) that she had driven across the marsh to Hartleys, where there was an auction sale; all the details of this she had completely forgotten, but she could recall quite clearly purchasing a set of gorgeous china which was still one of her proud delights, a perfect set of Crown Derby save that one plate was missing.

'How odd,' she remarked, 'that this Miss Lefain should collect china too, for it was at Hartleys that I purchased my dear old Derby service—I've never been able to match that plate—'.

'A plate was missing? I seem to remember,' said Clara. 'Didn't they say that it must be in the house somewhere and that it should be looked for?'

'I believe they did, but of course I never heard any more and that missing plate has annoyed me ever since. Who had Hartleys?'

'An old connoisseur, Sir James Sewell; I believe he was some relation to Miss Lefain, but I don't know—'

'I wonder if she has found the plate,' mused Miss Pym. 'I expect she has turned out and ransacked the whole place—'

'Why not trot over and ask?' suggested Mabel. 'It's not much use to her, if she has found it, one odd plate.'

'Don't be silly,' said Clara. 'Fancy going over the marshes, this weather, to ask about a plate missed all those years ago. I'm sure Martha wouldn't think of it—'

But Martha did think of it; she was rather fascinated by the idea; how queer and pleasant it would be if, after all these years, nearly a lifetime, she should find the Crown Derby plate, the loss of which had always irked her! And this hope did not seem so altogether fantastical, it was quite likely that old Miss Lefain, poking about in the ancient house, had found the missing piece.

And, of course, if she had, being a fellow-collector, she would be quite willing to part with it to complete the set.

Her cousin endeavoured to dissuade her; Miss Lefain, she declared, was a recluse, an odd creature who might greatly resent such a visit and such a request.

'Well, if she does I can but come away again,' smiled Miss Pym. 'I suppose she can't bite my head off, and I rather like meeting these curious types—we've got a love for old china in common, anyhow.'

'It seems so silly to think of it—after all these years—a plate!'

'A Crown Derby plate,' corrected Miss Pym. 'It is certainly strange that I didn't think of it before, but now that I have got it in my head I can't get it out. Besides,' she added hopefully, 'I might see the ghost.'

So full, however, were the days with pleasant local engagements that Miss Pym had no immediate chance of putting her scheme into practice; but she did not relinquish it, and she asked several different people what they knew about Hartleys and Miss Lefain.

And no one knew anything save that the house was supposed to be haunted and the owner 'cracky'.

'Is there a story?' asked Miss Pym, who associated ghosts with neat tales into which they fitted as exactly as nuts into shells.

But she was always told—'Oh, no, there isn't a story, no one knows anything about the place, don't know how the idea got about; old Sewell was half-crazy, I believe, he was buried in the garden and that gives a house a nasty name—'

'Very unpleasant,' said Martha Pym, undisturbed.

This ghost seemed too elusive for her to track down; she would have to be content if she could recover the Crown Derby plate; for that at least she was determined to make a try and also to satisfy that faint tingling of curiosity roused in her by this talk about 'Hartleys' and the remembrance of that day, so long ago, when she had gone to the auction sale at the lonely old house.

So the first free afternoon, while Mabel and Clara were comfortably taking their afternoon repose, Martha Pym, who was of a more lively habit, got out her little governess cart and dashed away across the Essex flats.

She had taken minute directions with her, but she had soon lost her way.

Under the wintry sky, which looked as grey and hard as metal, the marshes stretched bleakly to the horizon, the olive-brown broken reeds were harsh as scars on the saffron-tinted bogs, where the sluggish waters that rose so high in winter were filmed over with the first stillness of a frost; the air was cold but not keen, everything was damp; faintest of mists blurred the black outlines of trees that rose stark from the ridges above the stagnant dykes; the flooded fields were haunted by black birds and white birds, gulls and crows, whining above the long ditch grass and wintry wastes.

Miss Pym stopped the little horse and surveyed this spectral scene, which had a certain relish about it to one sure to return to a homely village, a cheerful house and good company.

A withered and bleached old man, in colour like the dun landscape, came along the road between the sparse alders.

Miss Pym, buttoning up her coat, asked the way to 'Hartley' as he passed her; he told her, straight on, and she proceeded, straight indeed across the road that went with undeviating length across the marshes.

'Of course,' thought Miss Pym, 'if you live in a place like this, you are bound to invent ghosts.'

The house sprang up suddenly on a knoll ringed with rotting trees, encompassed by an old brick wall that the perpetual damp had overrun with lichen, blue, green, white colours of decay.

Hartleys, no doubt, there was no other residence of human being in sight in all the wide expanse; besides, she could remember it, surely, after all this time, the sharp rising out of the marsh, the colony of tall trees, but then fields and trees had been green and bright—there had been no water on the flats, it had been summer-time.

'She certainly,' thought Miss Pym, 'must be crazy to live here. And I rather doubt if I shall get my plate.'

She fastened up the good little horse by the garden gate which stood negligently ajar and entered; the garden itself was so neglected that it was quite surprising to see a trim appearance in the house, curtains at the window and a polish on the brass door knocker, which must have been recently rubbed there, considering the taint in the sea damp which rusted and rotted everything.

It was a square-built, substantial house with 'nothing wrong with it but the situation,' Miss Pym decided, though it was not very attractive, being built of that drab plastered stone so popular a hundred years ago, with flat windows and door, while one side was gloomily shaded by a large evergreen tree of the cypress variety which gave a blackish tinge to that portion of the garden.

There was no pretence at flower-beds nor any manner of cultivation in this garden where a few rank weeds and straggling bushes matted together above the dead grass; on the enclosing wall, which appeared to have been built high as protection against the ceaseless winds that swung along the flats, were the remains of fruit trees; their crucified branches, rotting under the great nails that held them up, looked like the skeletons of those who had died in torment.

Miss Pym took in these noxious details as she knocked firmly at the door; they did not depress her; she merely felt extremely sorry for anyone who could live in such a place.

She noticed, at the far end of the garden, in the corner of the wall, a headstone showing above the sodden colourless grass, and remembered what she had been told about the old antiquary being buried there, in the grounds of Hartleys.

As the knock had no effect she stepped back and looked at the house; it was certainly inhabited—with those neat windows, white curtains and drab blinds all pulled to precisely the same level.

And when she brought her glance back to the door she saw that it had been opened and that someone, considerably obscured by the darkness of the passage, was looking at her intently.

'Good afternoon,' said Miss Pym cheerfully. 'I just thought that I would call to see Miss Lefain—it is Miss Lefain, isn't it?'

'It's my house,' was the querulous reply.

Martha Pym had hardly expected to find any servants here, though the old lady must, she thought, work pretty hard to keep the house so clean and tidy as it appeared to be.

'Of course,' she replied. 'May I come in? I'm Martha Pym, staying with the Wyntons, I met you there—'

'Do come in,' was the faint reply. 'I get so few people to visit me, I'm really very lonely.'

'I don't wonder,' thought Miss Pym; but she had resolved to take no notice of any eccentricity on the part of her hostess, and so she entered the house with her usual agreeable candour and courtesy.

The passage was badly lit, but she was able to get a fair idea of Miss Lefain; her first impression was that this poor creature was most dreadfully old, older than any human being had the right to be, why, she felt young in comparison—so faded, feeble, and pallid was Miss Lefain.

She was also monstrously fat; her gross, flaccid figure was shapeless and she wore a badly cut, full dress of no colour at all, but stained with earth and damp where Miss Pym supposed she had been doing futile gardening; this gown was doubtless designed to disguise her stoutness, but had been so carelessly pulled about that it only added to it, being rucked and rolled 'all over the place' as Miss Pym put it to herself.

Another ridiculous touch about the appearance of the poor old lady was her short hair; decrepit as she was, and lonely as she lived she had actually had her scanty relics of white hair cropped round her shaking head.

'Dear me, dear me,' she said in her thin treble voice. 'How very kind of you to come. I suppose you prefer the parlour? I generally sit in the garden.'

'The garden? But not in this weather?'

'I get used to the weather. You've no idea how used one gets to the weather.'

'I suppose so,' conceded Miss Pym doubtfully. 'You don't live here quite alone, do you?'

'Quite alone, lately. I had a little company, but she was taken away, I'm sure I don't know where. I haven't been able to find a trace of her anywhere,' replied the old lady peevishly.

'Some wretched companion that couldn't stick it, I suppose,' thought Miss Pym. 'Well, I don't wonder—but someone ought to be here to look after her.'

They went into the parlour, which, the visitor was dismayed to see, was without a fire but otherwise well kept.

And there, on dozens of shelves was a choice array of china at which Martha Pym's eyes glistened.

'Aha!' cried Miss Lefain. 'I see you've noticed my treasures! Don't you envy me? Don't you wish that you had some of those pieces?'

Martha Pym certainly did and she looked eagerly and greedily round the walls, tables, and cabinets while the old woman followed her with little thin squeals of pleasure.

It was a beautiful little collection, most choicely and elegantly arranged, and Martha thought it marvellous that this feeble ancient creature should be able to keep it in such precise order as well as doing her own housework.

'Do you really do everything yourself here and live quite alone?' she asked, and she shivered even in her thick coat and wished that Miss Lefain's energy had risen to a fire, but then probably she lived in the kitchen, as these lonely eccentrics often did.

'There was someone,' answered Miss Lefain cunningly, 'but I had to send her away. I told you she's gone, I can't find her, and I am so glad. Of course,' she added wistfully, 'it leaves me very lonely, but then I couldn't stand her impertinence any longer. She used to say that it was her house and her collection of china! Would you believe it? She used to try to chase me away from looking at my own things!'

'How very disagreeable,' said Miss Pym, wondering which of the two women had been crazy. 'But hadn't you better get someone else.'

'Oh, no,' was the jealous answer. 'I would rather be alone with my things, I daren't leave the house for fear someone takes them away—there was a dreadful time once when an auction sale was held here—'

'Were you here then?' asked Miss Pym; but indeed she looked old enough to have been anywhere.

'Yes, of course,' Miss Lefain replied rather peevishly and Miss Pym decided that she must be a relation of old Sir James Sewell. Clara and Mabel had been very foggy about it all. 'I was very busy hiding all the china—but one set they got—a Crown Derby tea service—'

'With one plate missing!' cried Martha Pym. 'I bought it, and do you know, I was wondering if you'd found it—'

'I hid it,' piped Miss Lefain.

'Oh, you did, did you? Well, that's rather funny behaviour. Why did you hide the stuff away instead of buying it?'

'How could I buy what was mine?'

'Old Sir James left it to you, then?' asked Martha Pym, feeling very muddled.

'She bought a lot more,' squeaked Miss Lefain, but Martha Pym tried to keep her to the point.

'If you've got the plate,' she insisted, 'you might let me have it—I'll pay quite handsomely, it would be so pleasant to have it after all these years.'

'Money is no use to me,' said Miss Lefain mournfully. 'Not a bit of use. I can't leave the house or the garden.'

'Well, you have to live, I suppose,' replied Martha Pym cheerfully. 'And, do you know, I'm afraid you are getting rather morbid and dull, living here all alone—you really ought to have a fire—why, it's just on Christmas and very damp.'

'I haven't felt the cold for a long time,' replied the other; she seated herself with a sigh on one of the horsehair chairs and Miss Pym noticed with a start that her feet were covered only by a pair of white stockings; 'one of those nasty health fiends,' thought Miss Pym, 'but she doesn't look too well for all that.'

'So you don't think that you could let me have the plate?' she asked briskly, walking up and down, for the dark, neat, clean parlour was very cold indeed, and she thought that she couldn't stand this much longer; as there seemed no sign of tea or anything pleasant and comfortable she had really better go.

'I might let you have it,' sighed Miss Lefain, 'since you've been so kind as to pay me a visit. After all, one plate isn't much use, is it?'

'Of course not, I wonder you troubled to hide it—'

'I couldn't *bear*,' wailed the other, 'to see the things going out of the house!'

Martha Pym couldn't stop to go into all this; it was quite clear that the old lady was very eccentric indeed and that nothing very much could be done with her; no wonder that she had 'dropped out' of everything and that no one ever saw her or knew anything about her, though Miss Pym felt that some effort ought really to be made to save her from herself.

'Wouldn't you like a run in my little governess cart?' she suggested. 'We might go to tea with the Wyntons on the way back, they'd be delighted to see you, and I really think that you do want taking out of yourself.'

'I was taken out of myself some time ago,' replied Miss Lefain. 'I really was, and I couldn't leave my things—though,' she added with pathetic gratitude, 'it is very, very kind of you—'

'Your things would be quite safe, I'm sure,' said Martha Pym, humouring her. 'Who ever would come up here, this hour of a winter's day?'

'They do, oh, they do! And *she* might come back, prying and nosing and saying that it was all hers, all my beautiful china, hers!'

Miss Lefain squealed in her agitation and rising up, ran round the wall fingering with flaccid yellow hands the brilliant glossy pieces on the shelves.

'Well, then, I'm afraid that I must go, they'll be expecting me, and it's quite a long ride; perhaps some other time you'll come and see us?'

'Oh, must you go?' quavered Miss Lefain dolefully. 'I do like a little company now and then and I trusted you from the first—the others, when they do come, are always after my things and I have to frighten them away!'

'Frighten them away!' replied Martha Pym. 'However do you do that?'

'It doesn't seem difficult, people are so easily frightened, aren't they?'

Miss Pym suddenly remembered that Hartleys had the reputation of being haunted—perhaps the queer old thing played on that; the lonely house with the grave in the garden was dreary enough around which to create a legend.

'I suppose you've never seen a ghost?' she asked pleasantly. 'I'd rather like to see one, you know—'

'There is no one here but myself,' said Miss Lefain.

'So you've never seen anything? I thought it must be all nonsense. Still, I do think it rather melancholy for you to live here all alone—'

Miss Lefain sighed:

'Yes, it's very lonely. Do stay and talk to me a little longer.' Her whistling voice dropped cunningly. 'And I'll give you the Crown Derby plate!'

'Are you sure you've really got it?' Miss Pym asked.

'I'll show you.'

Fat and waddling as she was, she seemed to move very lightly as she slipped in front of Miss Pym and conducted her from the room, going slowly up the stairs—such a gross odd figure in that clumsy dress with the fringe of white hair hanging on to her shoulders.

The upstairs of the house was as neat as the parlour, everything well in its place; but there was no sign of occupancy; the beds were covered with dust sheets, there were no lamps or fires set ready. 'I suppose,' said Miss Pym to herself, 'she doesn't care to show me where she really lives.'

But as they passed from one room to another, she could not help saying:

'Where do *you* live, Miss Lefain?'

'Mostly in the garden,' said the other.

Miss Pym thought of those horrible health huts that some people indulged in.

'Well, sooner you than I,' she replied cheerfully.

In the most distant room of all, a dark, tiny closet, Miss Lefain opened a deep cupboard and brought out a Crown Derby plate which her guest received with a spasm of joy, for it was actually that missing from her cherished set.

'It's very good of you,' she said in delight. 'Won't you take something for it, or let me do something for you?'

'You might come and see me again,' replied Miss Lefain wistfully.

'Oh, yes, of course I should like to come and see you again.'

But now that she had got what she had really come for, the plate, Martha Pym wanted to be gone; it was really very dismal and depressing in the house and she began to notice a fearful smell—the place had been shut up too long, there was something damp rotting somewhere, in this horrid little dark closet no doubt.

'I really must be going,' she said hurriedly.

Miss Lefain turned as if to cling to her, but Martha Pym moved quickly away.

'Dear me,' wailed the old lady. 'Why are you in such haste?'

'There's—a smell,' murmured Miss Pym rather faintly.

She found herself hastening down the stairs, with Miss Lefain complaining behind her.

'How peculiar people are—*she* used to talk of a smell—'

'Well, you must notice it yourself.'

Miss Pym was in the hall; the old woman had not followed her, but stood in the semi-darkness at the head of the stairs, a pale shapeless figure.

Martha Pym hated to be rude and ungrateful but she could not stay another moment; she hurried away and was in her cart in a moment—really—that smell—

'Good-bye!' she called out with false cheerfulness, 'and thank you *so* much!'

There was no answer from the house.

Miss Pym drove on; she was rather upset and took another way than that by which she had come, a way that led past a little house raised above the marsh; she was glad to think that the poor old creature at Hartleys had such near neighbours, and she reined up the horse, dubious as to whether she should call someone and tell them that poor old Miss Lefain really wanted a little looking after, alone in a house like that, and plainly not quite right in her head.

A young woman, attracted by the sound of the governess cart, came to the door of the house and seeing Miss Pym called out, asking if she wanted the keys of the house?

'What house?' asked Miss Pym.

'Hartleys, mum, they don't put a board out, as no one is likely to pass, but it's to be sold. Miss Lefain wants to sell or let it—'

'I've just been up to see her—'

'Oh, no, mum—she's been away a year, abroad somewhere, couldn't stand the place, it's been empty since then, I just run in every day and keep things tidy—'

Loquacious and curious the young woman had come to the fence; Miss Pym had stopped her horse.

'Miss Lefain is there now,' she said. 'She must have just come back—'

'She wasn't there this morning, mum, 'tisn't likely she'd come, either—fair scared she was, mum, fair chased away, didn't dare move her china. Can't say I've noticed anything myself, but I never stay long—and there's a smell—'

'Yes,' murmured Martha Pym faintly, 'there's a smell. What—what—chased her away?'

The young woman, even in that lonely place, lowered her voice.

'Well, as you aren't thinking of taking the place, she got an idea in her head that old Sir James—well, he couldn't bear to leave Hartleys, mum, he's buried in the garden, and she thought he was after her, chasing round them bits of china—'

'Oh!' cried Miss Pym.

'Some of it used to be his, she found a lot stuffed away, he said they were to be left in Hartleys, but Miss Lefain would have the things sold, I believe—that's years ago—'

'Yes, yes,' said Miss Pym with a sick look. 'You don't know what he was like, do you?'

'No, mum—but I've heard tell he was very stout and very old—I wonder who it was you saw up at Hartleys?'

Miss Pym took a Crown Derby plate from her bag.

'You might take that back when you go,' she whispered. 'I shan't want it, after all—'

Before the astonished young woman could answer Miss Pym had darted off across the marsh; that short hair, that earth-stained robe, the white socks, 'I generally live in the garden—'

Miss Pym drove away, breakneck speed, frantically resolving to mention to no one that she had paid a visit to Hartleys, nor lightly again to bring up the subject of ghosts.

She shook and shuddered in the damp, trying to get out of her clothes and her nostrils—that indescribable smell.

GREEN HOLLY

Elizabeth Bowen

FIRST PUBLISHED IN *THE LISTENER*,
21 DECEMBER 1944

Elizabeth Dorothea Cole Bowen was born in Dublin but lived for most of her life in England. Her most famous novels include *The Death of the Heart* (1938) and *The Heat of the Day* (1949), both of which explore the theme of loneliness – the former between the wars, and the latter, against the backdrop of the London Blitz. She did not use supernatural tropes in her novels, but was an enthusiastic writer of short ghost stories, seeing them as a perfect way of manifesting problems and uncertainties of the modern world. She explains in her introduction to Cynthia Asquith's anthology *The Second Ghost Book* (1952):

> Ghosts have grown up. Far behind lie their clanking and moaning days; they have laid aside their original bag of tricks – bleeding hands, luminous skulls and so on. Their manifestations are, like their personalities oblique and subtle, perfectly calculated to get the modern person under their skin. They abjure the over-fantastic and grotesque, operating, instead, through series of happenings whose horror lies in their being just, just out of the true... Ghosts draw us together:

one might leave it at that. Can there be something tonic about pure, active fear in these times of passive, confused oppression? It is nice to choose to be frightened, when one need not be. Or it may be that, deadened by information, we are glad of these awful, intent and nameless beings as to whom no information is to be had.

Mr. Rankstock entered the room with a dragging tread: nobody looked up or took any notice. With a muted groan, he dropped into an armchair—out of which he shot with a sharp yelp. He searched the seat of the chair, and extracted something. '*Your* holly, I think, Miss Bates,' he said, holding it out to her.

Miss Bates took a second or two to look up from her magazine. 'What?' she said. 'Oh, it must have fallen down from that picture. Put it back, please; we haven't got very much.'

'I regret,' interposed Mr. Winterslow, 'that we have any: it makes scratchy noises against the walls.'

'It is seasonable,' said Miss Bates firmly.

'You didn't do this to us last Christmas.'

'Last Christmas,' she said, 'I had Christmas leave. This year there seems to be none with berries: the birds have eaten them. If there were not a draught, the leaves would not scratch the walls. I cannot control the forces of nature, can I?'

'How should I know?' said Mr. Rankstock, lighting his pipe.

These three by now felt that, like Chevalier and his Old Dutch, they had been together for forty years: and to them it did seem a year too much. Actually, their confinement dated from 1940. They were Experts—in what, the Censor would not permit me to say. They were accounted for by their friends in

135

London as 'being somewhere off in the country, nobody knows where, doing something frightfully hush-hush, nobody knows what.' That is, they were accounted for in this manner if there were still anybody who still cared to ask; but on the whole they had dropped out of human memory. Their reappearances in their former circles were infrequent, ghostly and unsuccessful: their friends could hardly disguise their pity, and for their own part they had not a word to say. They had come to prefer to spend leaves with their families, who at least showed a flattering pleasure in their importance.

This Christmas, it so worked out that there was no question of leave for Mr. Rankstock, Mr. Winterslow or Miss Bates: with four others (now playing or watching pingpong in the next room) they composed in their high-grade way a skeleton staff. It may be wondered why, after years of proximity, they should continue to address one another so formally. They did not continue; they had begun again; in the matter of appellations, as in that of intimacy, they had by now, in fact by some time ago, completed the full circle. For some months, they could not recall in which year, Miss Bates had been engaged to Mr. Winterslow; before that, she had been extremely friendly with Mr. Rankstock. Mr. Rankstock's deviation towards one Carla (now at her pingpong in the next room) had been totally uninteresting to everybody; including, apparently, himself. If the war lasted, Carla might next year be called Miss Tongue; at present, Miss Bates was foremost in keeping her in her place by going on addressing her by her Christian name.

If this felt like their fortieth Christmas in each other's society, it was their first in these particular quarters. You would not have thought, as Mr. Rankstock said, that one country house could be much worse than any other; but this had proved, and was still proving, untrue. The Army, for reasons it failed to justify, wanted the house they had been in since 1940; so they—lock, stock and barrel and files and all—had been bundled into another one, six miles away. Since the move, tentative exploration (for they were none of them walkers) had established that they were now surrounded by rather more mud but fewer trees. What they did know was, their already sufficient distance from the market town with its bars and movies had now been added to by six miles. On the other side of their new home, which was called Mopsam Grange, there appeared to be nothing; unless, as Miss Bates suggested, swineherds, keeping their swine. Mopsam village contained villagers, evacuees, a church, a public-house on whose never-open door was chalked 'No Beer, No Matches, No Teas Served', and a vicar. The vicar had sent up a nice note, saying he was not clear whether Security regulations would allow him to call; and the doctor had been up once to lance one of Carla's boils.

Mopsam Grange was neither old nor new. It replaced—unnecessarily, they all felt—a house on this site that had been burned down. It had a Gothic porch and gables, french windows, bow windows, a conservatory, a veranda, a hall which, puce-and-buff tiled and pitch-pine-panelled, rose to a gallery: in fact, every advantage. Jackdaws fidgeted in its many chimneys—for it had, till the war, stood empty: one had not to ask why. The hot-water system made what Carla called rude noises, and was capricious in its supplies to the (only) two mahogany-rimmed baths. The electric light ran from a plant in the yard; if the batteries were not kept charged the light turned brown.

The three now sat in the drawing-room, on whose walls, mirrors and fitments, long since removed, left traces. There were, however, some pictures: General Montgomery (who had just shed his holly) and some Landseer engravings that had been found in an attic. Three electric bulbs, naked, shed light manfully; and in the grate the coal fire was doing far from badly. Miss Bates rose and stood twiddling the bit of holly. 'Something,' she said, 'has got to be done about this.' Mr. Winterslow and Mr. Rankstock, the latter sucking in his pipe, sank lower, between their shoulder-blades, in their respective armchairs. Miss Bates, having drawn a breath, took a running jump at a table, which she propelled across the floor with a grating sound. '*Achtung!*' she shouted at Mr. Rankstock, who, with an oath, withdrew his chair from her route. Having got the table under General Montgomery, Miss Bates—with a display of long, slender leg, clad in ribbed scarlet sports stockings, that was of interest to no one—mounted it, then proceeded to tuck the holly back into position over the General's frame. Meanwhile, Mr. Winterslow, choosing his moment, stealthily reached across her empty chair and possessed himself of her magazine.

What a hope!—Miss Bates was known to have eyes all the way down her spine. 'Damn you, Mr. Winterslow,' she said, 'put that down! Mr. Rankstock, interfere with Mr. Winterslow: Mr. Winterslow has taken my magazine!' She ran up and down the table like something in a cage; Mr. Rankstock removed his pipe from his mouth, dropped his head back, gazed up and said: 'Gad, Miss Bates; you look fine...'

'It's a pretty *old* magazine,' murmured Mr. Winterslow flicking the pages over.

'Well, *you're* pretty old,' she said. 'I hope Carla gets you!'

'Oh, I can do better, thank you; I've got a ghost.'

This confidence, however, was cut off by Mr. Rankstock's having burst into song. Holding his pipe at arm's length, rocking on his bottom in his armchair, he led them:

> "'Heigh-ho! sing Heigh-ho! unto the green holly:
> Most friendship is feigning, most loving mere folly—'"

"'*Mere folly, mere folly*,'" contributed Mr. Winterslow, picking up, joining in. Both sang:

> "'*Then, heigh-ho, the holly!*
> *This life is most jolly.*'"

'Now—*all*!' said Mr. Rankstock, jerking his pipe at Miss Bates. So all three went through it once more, with degrees of passion: Miss Bates, when others desisted, being left singing 'Heigh-ho! sing heigh-ho! sing—' all by herself. Next door, the pingpong came to an awestruck stop. 'At any rate,' said Mr. Rankstock, 'we all like Shakespeare.' Miss Bates, whose intelligence, like her singing, tonight seemed some way at the tail of the hunt, looked blank, began to get off the table, and said, 'But I thought that was a Christmas carol?'

Her companions shrugged and glanced at each other. Having taken her magazine away from Mr. Winterslow, she was once more settling down to it when she seemed struck. 'What was that you said, about you had got a ghost?'

Mr. Winterslow looked down his nose. 'At this early stage, I don't like to say very much. In fact, on the whole, forget it; if you don't mind—'

'Look,' Mr. Rankstock said, 'if you've started seeing things—'

'I am only sorry,' his colleague said, 'that I've spoke.'

'Oh no, you're not,' said Miss Bates, 'and we'd better know. Just what *is* fishy about this Grange?'

'There is nothing "fishy",' said Mr. Winterslow in a fastidious tone. It was hard, indeed, to tell from his manner whether he did or did not regret having made a start. He had reddened—but not, perhaps, wholly painfully—his eyes, now fixed on the fire, were at once bright and vacant; with unheeding, fumbling movements he got out a cigarette, lit it and dropped the match on the floor, to slowly burn one more hole in the fibre mat. Gripping the cigarette between tense lips, he first flung his arms out, as though casting off a cloak; then pressed both hands, clasped firmly, to the nerve-centre in the nape of his neck, as though to contain the sensation there. 'She was marvellous,' he brought out—'what I could see of her.'

'Don't talk with your cigarette in your mouth,' Miss Bates said. '—Young?'

'Adorably, not so very. At the same time, quite—oh well, you know what I mean.'

'Uh-hu,' said Miss Bates. 'And wearing—?'

'I am certain she had a feather boa.'

'You mean,' Mr. Rankstock said, 'that this brushed your face?'

'And when and where did this happen?' said Miss Bates with legal coldness.

Cross-examination, clearly, became more and more repugnant to Mr. Winterslow in his present mood. He shut his eyes, sighed bitterly, heaved himself from his chair, said: 'Oh, well—' and stood indecisively looking towards the door. 'Don't let us keep you,' said Miss Bates. 'But one thing I don't see is: if you're

140

being fed with beautiful thoughts, why you wanted to keep on taking my magazine?'

'I wanted to be distracted.'

'?'

'There *are* moments when I don't quite know where I am.'

'You surprise me,' said Mr. Rankstock.—'Good *God* man, what is the matter?' For Mr. Winterslow, like a man being swooped around by a bat, was revolving, staring from place to place high up round the walls of the gaunt, lit room. Miss Bates observed: 'Well, now we *have* started something.' Mr. Rankstock, considerably kinder, said: 'That is only Miss Bates's holly, flittering in the wind.'

Mr. Winterslow gulped. He walked to the inch of mirror propped on the mantelpiece and, as nonchalantly as possible, straightened his tie. Having done this, he said: 'But there isn't a wind tonight.'

The ghost hesitated in the familiar corridor. Her visibleness, even on Christmas Eve, was not under her own control; and now she had fallen in love again her dependence upon it began to dissolve in patches. This was a concentration of every feeling of the woman prepared to sail downstairs *en grande tenue*. Flamboyance and agitation were both present. But between these, because of her years of death, there cut an extreme anxiety: it was not merely a matter of, how was she? but of, *was* she—tonight—at all? Death had left her to be her own mirror; for into no other was she able to see.

For tonight, she had discarded the feather boa; it had been dropped into the limbo that was her wardrobe now. Her shoulders, she knew, were bare. Round their bareness shimmered a thousand evenings. Her own person haunted her—above her forehead, the crisped springy weight of her pompadour; round her feet the frou-frou of her skirts on a thick carpet; in her nostrils the scent from her corsage; up and down her forearm the glittery slipping of bracelets warmed by her own blood. It is the haunted who haunt.

There were lights in the house again. She had heard laughter, and there had been singing. From those few dim lights and untrue notes her senses, after their starvation, set going the whole old grand opera. She smiled, and moved down the corridor to the gallery, where she stood looking down into the hall. The tiles of the hall floor were as pretty as ever, as cold as ever, and bore, as always on Christmas Eve, the trickling pattern of dark blood. The figure of the man with the side of his head blown out lay as always, one foot just touching the lowest step of the stairs. It was too bad. She had been silly, but it could not be helped. They should not have shut her up in the country. How could she not make hay while the sun shone? The year round, no man except her husband, his uninteresting jealousy, his dull passion. Then, at Christmas, so many men that one did not know where to turn. The ghost, leaning further over the gallery, pouted down at the suicide. She said: 'You should have let me explain.' The man made no answer: he never had.

Behind a door somewhere downstairs, a racket was going on: the house sounded funny, there were no carpets. The morning-room door was flung open and four flushed people, headed by a young woman, charged out. They clattered across the man and the trickling pattern as though there were nothing there but the tiles. In the morning-room, she saw one small white ball trembling to stillness upon the floor. As the people rushed the stairs and fought for place in the gallery the ghost drew back—a purest act of repugnance, for this was not necessary. The young woman, to one of whose temples was strapped a cotton-wool pad, held her place and disappeared round a corner exulting: '*My* bath, *my* bath!' 'Then may you freeze in it, Carla!' returned the scrawniest of the defeated ones. The words pierced the ghost, who trembled—they did not know!

Who were they? She did not ask. She did not care. She never had been inquisitive: information had bored her. Her schooled lips had framed one set of questions, her eyes a consuming other. Now the mills of death with their catching wheels had stripped her of semblance, cast her forth on an everlasting holiday from pretence. She was left with—nay, had become—her obsession. Thus is it to be a ghost. The ghost fixed her eyes on the other, the drawing-room door. He had gone in there. He would have to come out again.

The handle turned; the door opened; Winterslow came out. He shut the door behind him, with the sedulous slowness of an uncertain man. He had been humming, and now, squaring his shoulders, began to sing, '... *Mere folly, mere folly*—' as he crossed the hall towards the foot of the staircase, obstinately never raising his eyes. 'So it is you,' breathed the ghost, with unheard softness. She gathered about her, with a gesture not less proud for being tormentedly uncertain, the total of her visibility—was it possible diamonds should not glitter now, on her rising-and-falling breast—and swept from the gallery to the head of the stairs.

Winterslow shivered violently, and looked up. He licked his lips. He said: 'This cannot go on.'

The ghost's eyes, with tender impartiality and mockery, from above swept Winterslow's face. The hair receding, the furrowed forehead, the tired sag of the jowl, the strain-reddened eyelids, the blue-shaved chin—nothing was lost on her, nothing broke the spell. With untroubled wonder she saw his handwoven tie, his coat pockets shapeless as saddle-bags, the bulging knees of his flannel trousers. Wonder went up in rhapsody: so much chaff in the fire. She never had had illusions: *the* illusion was all. Lovers cannot be choosers. He'd do. He would have to do.—'I know!' she agreed, with rapture, casting her hands together. 'We are mad—you and I. Oh, what is going to happen? I entreat you to leave this house tonight!'

Winterslow, in a dank, unresounding voice, said: 'And anyhow, what made you pick on me?'

'It's Kismet,' wailed the ghost zestfully. 'Why did you have to come here? Why you? I had been so peaceful, just like a little girl. People spoke of love, but I never knew what they meant. Oh, I could wish we had never met, you and I!'

Winterslow said: 'I have been here for three months; we have all of us been here, as a matter of fact. Why all this all of a sudden?'

She said: 'There's a Christmas Eve party, isn't there, going on? One Christmas Eve party, there was a terrible accident. Oh, comfort me! No one has understood.—Don't stand *there*; I can't bear it—not just *there*!'

Winterslow, whether he heard or not, cast a scared glance down at his feet, which were in slippers, then shifted a pace or two to the left. 'Let me up,' he said wildly. 'I tell you, I want my spectacles! I just want to get my spectacles. Let me by!'

'*Let* you up!' the ghost marvelled. 'But I am only waiting...'

She was more than waiting: she set up a sort of suction, an icy indrawing draught. Nor was this wholly psychic, for an isolated holly leaf of Miss Bates's, dropped at a turn of the staircase, twitched. And not, you could think, by chance did the electric light choose this moment for one of its brown fade-outs: gradually, the scene—the hall, the stairs and the gallery—faded under this fog-dark but glass-clear veil of hallucination. The feet of Winterslow, under remote control, began with knocking unsureness to mount the stairs. At their turn he staggered, steadied himself, and then stamped derisively upon the holly leaf. 'Bah,' he neighed—'*spectacles*!'

By the ghost now putting out everything, not a word could be dared.

'Where are you?'

Weakly, her dress rustled, three steps down: the rings on her hand knocked weakly over the panelling. 'Here, oh here,' she sobbed. 'Where I was before...'

'Hell,' said Miss Bates, who had opened the drawing-room door and was looking resentfully round the hall. 'This electric light.'

Mr. Rankstock, from inside the drawing-room, said: 'Find the man.'

'The man has gone to the village. Mr. Rankstock, if *you* were half a man—. Mr. Winterslow, what are you doing, kneeling down on the stairs? Have you come over funny? Really, this is the end.'

At the other side of a baize door, one of the installations began ringing. 'Mr. Rankstock,' Miss Bates yelled implacably, 'yours, this time.' Mr. Rankstock, with an expression of hatred, whipped out a pencil and pad and shambled across the hall.

Under cover of this Mr. Winterslow pushed himself upright, brushed his knees and began to descend the stairs, to confront his colleague's narrow but not unkind look. Weeks of exile from any hairdresser had driven Miss Bates to the Alice-in-Wonderland style: her snood, tied at the top, was now thrust back, adding inches to her pale, polished brow. Nicotine stained the fingers she closed upon Mr. Winterslow's elbow, propelling him back to the drawing-room. 'There is always drink,' she said. 'Come along.'

He said hopelessly: 'If you mean the bottle between the filing cabinets, I finished that when I had to work last night.—Look here, Miss Bates, why should she have picked on *me*?'

'It has been broken off, then?' said Miss Bates. 'I'm sorry for you, but I don't like your tone. I resent your attitude to my sex. For that matter, why did you pick on her? Romantic, nostalgic, Blue-Danube-fixated—hein? There's Carla, an understanding girl, unselfish, getting over her boils; there are Avice and Lettice, due back on Boxing Day. There is me, as you have ceased to observe. But oh dear no; *we* do not trail feather boas—'

'—She only wore that in the afternoon.'

'Now let me tell you something,' said Miss Bates. 'When I opened the door, just now, to have a look at the lights, what do you think *I* first saw there in the hall?'

'Me,' replied Mr. Winterslow, with returning assurance.

'*O-oh* no; oh indeed no,' said Miss Bates. 'You—why should I think twice of that, if you *were* striking attitudes on the stairs? You?—no, I saw your enchanting inverse. Extended, and it is true stone dead, I saw the man of my dreams. From his attitude, it was clear he had died for love. There were three pearl studs in his boiled shirt, and his white tie must have been tied in heaven. And the hand that had dropped the pistol had dropped a white rose; it lay beside him brown and crushed from having been often kissed. The ideality of those kisses, for the last of which I arrived too late—' here Miss Bates beat her fist against the bow of her snood—'will haunt, and by haunting satisfy me. The destruction of his features, before I saw them, made their former perfection certain, where I am concerned.—And here I am, left, left, left, to watch dust gather on Mr. Rankstock and you; to watch—yes, I who saw in a flash the ink-black perfection of *his* tailoring—mildew form on those clothes that you never change; to remember how both of you had in common that way of blowing your noses before you kissed me. He had been deceived—hence the shot, hence the fall. But who was *she*, your feathered friend, to deceive him? Who could have deceived him more superbly than I?—*I* could be fatal,' moaned Miss Bates, pacing the drawing-room, '*I* could be fatal—only give me a break!'

'Well, I'm sorry,' said Mr. Winterslow, 'but really, what can I do, or poor Rankstock do? We are just ourselves.'

'You put the thing in a nutshell,' said Miss Bates. 'Perhaps I could bear it if you just got your hairs cut.'

'If it comes to that, Miss Bates, you might get yours set.'

Mr. Rankstock's re-entry into the drawing-room—this time with brisker step, for a nice little lot of new trouble was brewing up—synchronised with the fall of the piece of holly, again, from the General's frame to the Rankstock chair. This time he saw it in time. '*Your* holly, I think, Miss Bates,' he said, holding it out to her.

'We must put it back,' said Miss Bates. 'We haven't got very much.'

'I cannot see,' said Mr. Winterslow, 'why we should have any. I don't see the point of holly without berries.'

'The birds have eaten them,' said Miss Bates. 'I cannot control the forces of nature, can I?'

'*Then heigh-ho! sing heigh-ho!*—' Mr. Rankstock led off.

'Yes,' she said, 'let us have that pretty carol again.'

CHRISTMAS RE-UNION

Andrew Caldecott

PUBLISHED IN *NOT EXACTLY GHOSTS* (1947)

Sir Andrew Caldecott (1884–1951) began writing ghost stories after retiring from the colonial civil service in 1944. He was born in Kent, the son of a clergyman, and joined the Malayan civil service in 1907. During his long career he held the governorships of Hong Kong and Ceylon (now Sri Lanka). He is credited with having helped to smooth the way for independence in Ceylon, which it attained in 1948. He published two volumes of ghost stories, in 1947 and 1948, and his work is thought to be somewhat reminiscent of the great master of the genre, M. R. James. 'Christmas Re-union' is actually based on an idea that James described in his essay 'Stories I have tried to write'.

I

'I cannot explain what exactly it is about him; but I don't like your Mr. Clarence Love, and I'm sorry that you ever asked him to stay.'

Thus Richard Dreyton to his wife Elinor on the morning of Christmas Eve.

'But one must remember the children, Richard. You know what marvellous presents he gives them.'

'Much too marvellous. He spoils them. Yet you'll have noticed that none of them likes him. Children have a wonderful intuition in regard to the character of grown-ups.'

'What on earth are you hinting about his character? He's a very nice man.'

Dreyton shuffled off his slippers in front of the study fire and began putting on his boots.

'I wonder, darling, whether you noticed his face just now at breakfast, when he opened that letter with the Australian stamps on?'

'Yes; he did seem a bit upset: but not more so than you when you get my dressmaker's bill!'

Mrs. Dreyton accompanied this sally with a playful pat on her husband's back as he leant forward to do up his laces.

'Well, Elinor, all that I can say is that there's something very fishy about his antipodean history. At five-and-twenty, he left

151

England a penniless young man and, heigh presto! he returns a stinking plutocrat at twenty-eight. And how? What he's told you doesn't altogether tally with what he's told me; but, cutting out the differences, his main story is that he duly contacted old Nelson Joy, his maternal uncle, whom he went out to join, and that they went off together, prospecting for gold. They struck it handsomely; and then the poor old uncle gets a heart-stroke or paralysis, or something, in the bush, and bids Clarence leave him there to die and get out himself before the food gives out. Arrived back in Sydney, Clarence produces a will under which he is the sole beneficiary, gets the Court to presume old Joy's death, and bunks back here with the loot.'

Mrs. Dreyton frowned. 'I can see nothing wrong or suspicious about the story,' she said, 'but only in your telling of it.'

'No! No! In his telling of it. He never gets the details quite the same twice running, and I'm certain that he gave a different topography to their prospecting expedition this year from what he did last. It's my belief that he did the uncle in, poor old chap!'

'Don't be so absurd, Richard; and please remember that he's our guest, and that we must be hospitable: especially at Christmas. Which reminds me: on your way to office, would you mind looking in at Harridge's and making sure that they haven't forgotten our order for their Santa Claus tomorrow? He's to be here at seven; then to go on to the Simpsons at seven-thirty, and to end up at the Joneses at eight. It's lucky our getting three households to share the expenses: Harridge's charge each of us only half their catalogued fee. If they could possibly send us the same Father Christmas as last year it would be splendid. The children adored him. Don't forget to say, too, that he will find all the crackers, hats, musical toys and presents

152

inside the big chest in the hall. Just the same as last year. What should we do nowadays without the big stores? One goes to them for everything.'

'We certainly do,' Dreyton agreed; 'and I can't see the modern child putting up with the amateur Father Christmas we used to suffer from. I shall never forget the annual exhibition Uncle Bertie used to make of himself, or the slippering I got when I stuck a darning-needle into his behind under pretence that I wanted to see if he was real! Well, so long, old girl: no, I won't forget to call in at Harridge's.'

2

By the time the festive Christmas supper had reached the dessert stage, Mrs. Dreyton fully shared her husband's regret that she had ever asked Clarence Love to be of the party. The sinister change that had come over him on receipt of the letter from Australia became accentuated on the later arrival of a telegram which, he said, would necessitate his leaving towards the end of the evening to catch the eight-fifteen northbound express from King's Pancras. His valet had already gone ahead with the luggage and, as it had turned so foggy, he had announced his intention of following later by Underground, in order to avoid the possibility of being caught in a traffic-jam.

It is strange how sometimes the human mind can harbour simultaneously two entirely contradictory emotions. Mrs. Dreyton was consumed with annoyance that any guest of hers should be so inconsiderate as to terminate his stay in the middle of a Christmas party; but was, at the same time, impatient to be rid of such a skeleton at the feast. One of the things that she had found attractive in Clarence Love had been an unfailing fund of small talk, which, if not brilliant, was at any rate bright and breezy. He possessed, also, a pleasant and frequent smile and, till now, had always been assiduous in his attention to her conversation. Since yesterday, however, he had turned silent, inattentive, and dour in expression. His presentation to her of a lovely emerald brooch had been unaccompanied by any greeting beyond an unflattering and perfunctory 'Happy Christmas!' He had also proved unforgivably oblivious of the mistletoe, beneath which, with a careful carelessness, she stationed herself when she heard him coming down to breakfast. It was, indeed, quite mortifying; and, when her husband described the guest as a busted balloon, she had neither the mind nor the heart to gainsay him.

Happily for the mirth and merriment of the party Dreyton seemed to derive much exhilaration from the dumb discomfiture of his wife's friend, and Elinor had never seen or heard her husband in better form. He managed, too, to infect the children with his own ebullience; and even Miss Potterby (the governess) reciprocated his fun. Even before the entry of Father Christmas it had thus become a noisy, and almost rowdy, company.

Father Christmas's salutation, on arrival, was in rhymed verse and delivered in the manner appropriate to pantomime. His lines ran thus:

> To Sons of Peace
> Yule brings release
> From worry at this tide;
> But men of crime

This holy time
Their guilty heads need hide.
So never fear,
Ye children dear,
But innocent sing 'Nowell';
For the Holy Rood
Shall save the good,
And the bad be burned in hell.
This is my carol
And Nowell my parole.

There was clapping of hands at this, for there is nothing children enjoy so much as mummery; especially if it be slightly mysterious. The only person who appeared to dislike the recitation was Love, who was seen to stop both ears with his fingers at the end of the first verse and to look ill. As soon as he had made an end of the prologue, Santa Claus went ahead with his distribution of gifts, and made many a merry quip and pun. He was quick in the uptake, too; for the children put to him many a poser, to which a witty reply was always ready. The minutes indeed slipped by all too quickly for all of them, except Love, who kept glancing uncomfortably at his wrist-watch and was plainly in a hurry to go. Hearing him mutter that it was time for him to be off, Father Christmas walked to his side and bade him pull a farewell cracker. Having done so, resentfully it seemed, he was asked to pull out the motto and read it. His hands were now visibly shaking, and his voice seemed to have caught their infection. Very falteringly, he managed to stammer out the two lines of doggerel:

Re-united heart to heart
Love and joy shall never part.

'And now,' said Father Christmas, 'I must be making for the next chimney; and, on my way, sir, I will see you into the Underground.'

So saying he took Clarence Love by the left arm and led him with mock ceremony to the door, where he turned and delivered this epilogue:

Ladies and Gentlemen, good-night!
Let not darkness you affright.
Aught of evil here today
Santa Claus now bears away.

At this point, with sudden dramatic effect, he clicked off the electric light switch by the door; and, by the time Dreyton had groped his way to it in the darkness and turned it on again, the parlour-maid (who was awaiting Love's departure in the hall) had let both him and Father Christmas out into the street.

'Excellent!' Mrs. Dreyton exclaimed, 'quite excellent! One can always depend on Harridge's. It wasn't the same man as they sent last year; but quite as good, and more original, perhaps.'

'I'm glad he's taken Mr. Love away,' said young Harold.

'Yes,' Dorothy chipped in; 'he's been beastly all day, and yesterday, too: and his presents aren't nearly as expensive as last year.'

'Shut up, you spoilt children!' the father interrupted. 'I must admit, though, that the fellow was a wet blanket this evening. What was that nonsense he read out about reunion?'

Miss Potterby had developed a pedagogic habit of clearing her throat audibly, as a signal demanding her pupils' attention to some impending announcement. She did it now, and parents as well as children looked expectantly towards her.

'The motto as read by Mr. Love,' she declared, 'was so palpably inconsequent that I took the liberty of appropriating it when he laid the slip of paper back on the table. Here it is, and this is how it actually reads:

> Be united heart to heart,
> Love and joy shall never part.

That makes sense, if it doesn't make poetry. Mr. Love committed the error of reading "be united" as "reunited" and of not observing the comma between the two lines.'

'Thank you, Miss Potterby; that, of course, explains it. How clever of you to have spotted the mistake and tracked it down!'

Thus encouraged, Miss Potterby proceeded to further corrective edification.

'You remarked just now, Mrs. Dreyton, that the gentleman impersonating Father Christmas had displayed originality. His prologue and epilogue, however, were neither of them original, but corrupted versions of passages which you will find in Professor Borleigh's Synopsis of Nativity, Miracle and Morality Plays, published two years ago. I happen to be familiar with the subject, as the author is a first cousin of mine, once removed.'

'How interesting!' Dreyton here broke in; 'and now, Miss Potterby, if you will most kindly preside at the piano, we will dance Sir Roger de Coverley. Come on, children, into the drawing-room.'

3

On Boxing Day there was no post and no paper. Meeting Mrs. Simpson in the Park that afternoon, Mrs. Dreyton was surprised to hear that Father Christmas had kept neither of his two other engagements. 'It must have been that horrid fog,' she suggested; 'but what a shame! He was even better than last year:' by which intelligence Mrs. Simpson seemed little comforted.

Next morning—the second after Christmas—there were two letters on the Dreytons' breakfast-table, and both were from Harridge's.

The first conveyed that firm's deep regret that their representative should have been prevented from carrying out his engagements in Pentland Square on Christmas night owing to dislocation of traffic caused by the prevailing fog.

'But he kept ours all right,' Mrs. Dreyton commented. 'I feel so sorry for the Simpsons and the Joneses.'

The second letter cancelled the first, 'which had been written in unfortunate oversight of the cancellation of the order'.

'What on earth does that mean?' Mrs. Dreyton ejaculated.

'Ask me another!' returned her husband. 'Got their correspondence mixed up, I suppose.'

In contrast to the paucity of letters, the morning newspapers seemed unusually voluminous and full of pictures. Mrs. Dreyton's choice of what to read in them was not that of a highbrow. The headline that attracted her first attention ran 'XMAS ON UNDERGROUND', and, among other choice items, she learned how, at Pentland Street Station (their own nearest), a man dressed as Santa Claus had been seen to guide and support an invalid, or possibly tipsy, companion down the long escalator. The red coat, mask and beard were afterwards found discarded in a passage leading to the emergency staircase, so that even Santa's sobriety might be called into question. She was just about to retail this interesting intelligence to her husband when, laying down his own paper, he stared curiously at her and muttered 'Good God!'

'What on earth's the matter, dear?'

'A very horrible thing, Elinor. Clarence Love has been killed! Listen;' here he resumed his paper and began to read aloud: "The body of the man who fell from the Pentland Street platform on Christmas night in front of an incoming train has been identified as that of Mr. Clarence Love, of 11 Playfair Mansions. There was a large crowd of passengers on the platform at the time, and it is conjectured that he fell backwards off it while turning to expostulate with persons exerting pressure at his back. Nobody, however, in the crush, could have seen the exact circumstances of the said fatality."'

'Hush, dear! Here come the children. They mustn't know, of course. We can talk about it afterwards.'

Dreyton, however, could not wait to talk about it afterwards. The whole of the amateur detective within him had been aroused, and, rising early from the breakfast-table, he journeyed by tube to Harridge's, where he was soon interviewing a departmental sub-manager. No: there was no possibility of one of their representatives having visited Pentland Square on Christmas evening. Our Mr. Droper had got hung up in the Shenton Street traffic-block until it was too late to keep his engagements there. He had come straight back to his rooms. In any case, he would not have called at Mr. Dreyton's residence in view of the cancellation of the order the previous day. Not cancelled? But he took down the telephone message himself. Yes: here was the entry in the register. Then it must have been the work of some mischief-maker; it was certainly a gentleman's, and not a lady's voice. Nobody except he and Mr. Droper knew of the engagement at their end, so the practical joker must have derived his knowledge of it from somebody in Mr. Dreyton's household.

This was obviously sound reasoning and, on his return home, Dreyton questioned Mrs. Timmins, the cook, in the matter. She was immediately helpful and forthcoming. One of them insurance gents had called on the morning before Christmas and had been told that none of us wanted no policies or such like. He had then turned conversational and asked what sort of goings-on there would be here for Christmas. Nothing, he was told, except old Father Christmas, as usual, out of Harridge's shop. Then he asked about visitors in the house, and was told as there were none except Mr. Love, who, judging by the tip what he had given Martha when he stayed last in the house, was a wealthy and open-handed gentleman. Little did she think when she spoke those words as Mr. Love would forget to give any tips or boxes at Christmas, when they were most natural and proper. But perhaps he would think better on it by the New Year and send a postal order. Dreyton thought it unlikely, but deemed it unnecessary at this juncture to inform Mrs. Timmins of the tragedy reported in the newspaper.

At luncheon Mrs. Dreyton found her husband unusually taciturn and preoccupied; but, by the time they had come to the cheese, he announced importantly that he had made up his mind to report immediately to the police certain information that had come into his possession. Miss Potterby and the children looked suitably impressed, but knew better than to court a snub by asking questions. Mrs. Dreyton took the cue admirably by replying: 'Of course, Richard, you must do your duty!'

4

The inspector listened intently and jotted down occasional notes. At the end of the narration, he complimented the informant by asking whether he had formed any theory regarding the facts he reported. Dreyton most certainly had. That was why he had been so silent and absent-minded at lunch. His solution, put much more briefly than he expounded it to the inspector, was as follows.

Clarence Love had abandoned his uncle and partner in the Australian bush. Having returned to civilisation, got the Courts to presume the uncle's death, and taken probate of the will under which he was sole inheritor, Love returned to England a wealthy and still youngish man. The uncle, however (this was Dreyton's theory), did not die after his nephew's desertion, but was found and tended by bushmen. Having regained his power of locomotion, he trekked back to Sydney, where he discovered himself legally dead and his property appropriated by Love and removed to England. Believing his nephew to have compassed his death, he resolved to take revenge into his own hands. Having despatched a cryptic letter to Love containing dark hints of impending doom, he sailed for the Old Country and ultimately tracked Love down to the Dreytons' abode. Then, having in the guise of a travelling insurance agent ascertained the family's programme for Christmas Day,

he planned his impersonation of Santa Claus. That his true
identity, revealed by voice and accent, did not escape his victim
was evidenced by the latter's nervous misreading of the motto
in the cracker. Whether Love's death in the Underground
was due to actual murder or to suicide enforced by despair
and remorse, Dreyton hazarded no guess: either was possible
under his theory.

The inspector's reception of Dreyton's hypothesis was less
enthusiastic than his wife's.

'If you'll excuse me, Mr. Dreyton,' said the former, 'you've
built a mighty lot on dam' little. Still, it's ingenious and no
mistake. I'll follow your ideas up and, if you'll call in a week's
time, I may have something to tell you and one or two things,
perhaps, to ask.'

'Why darling, how wonderful!' Mrs. Dreyton applauded.
'Now that you've pieced the bits together so cleverly the thing's
quite obvious, isn't it? What a horrible thing to have left poor
old Mr. Joy to die all alone in the jungle! I never really liked
Clarence, and am quite glad now that he's dead. But of course
we mustn't tell the children!'

Inquiries of the Australian Police elicited the intelligence
that the presumption of Mr. Joy's death had been long since
confirmed by the discovery of his remains in an old prospecting pit. There were ugly rumours and suspicions against his
nephew but no evidence on which to support them. On being
thus informed by the inspector Dreyton amended his theory
to the extent that the impersonator of Father Christmas must
have been not Mr. Joy himself, as he was dead, but a bosom
friend determined to avenge him. This substitution deprived
the cracker episode, on which Dreyton had imagined his whole

story, of all relevance; and the inspector was quite frank about his disinterest in the revised version.

Mrs. Dreyton also rejected it. Her husband's original theory seemed to her more obviously right and conclusive even than before. The only amendment required, and that on a mere matter of detail, was to substitute Mr. Joy's ghost for Mr. Joy: though of course one mustn't tell the children.

'But,' her husband remonstrated, 'you know that I don't believe in ghosts.'

'No, but your aunt Cecilia does; and she is such a clever woman. By the way, she called in this morning and left you a book to look at.'

'A book?'

'Yes, the collected ghost stories of M. R. James.'

'But the stupid old dear knows that I have them all in the original editions.'

'So she said: but she wants you to read the author's epilogue to the collection which, she says, is most entertaining. It's entitled "Stories I have tried to write". She said that she'd side-lined a passage that might interest you. The book's on that table by you. No, not that: the one with the black cover.'

Dreyton picked it up, found the marked passage and read it aloud.

> There may be possibilities too in the Christmas cracker if the right people pull it and if the motto which they find inside has the right message on it. They will probably leave the party early, pleading indisposition; but very likely a previous engagement of long standing would be the more truthful excuse.

'There is certainly,' Dreyton commented, 'some resemblance between James's idea and our recent experience. But he could have made a perfectly good yarn out of that theme without introducing ghosts.'

His wife's mood at that moment was for compromise rather than controversy.

'Well, darling,' she temporised, 'perhaps not exactly ghosts.'

A CHRISTMAS MEETING

Rosemary Timperley

FIRST PUBLISHED IN *THE SECOND GHOST BOOK* (ED. CYNTHIA ASQUITH, 1952)

Rosemary Kenyon Timperley (1920–1988) was born in Crouch End in North London. She was working as a teacher when her first story was published in *Illustrated* magazine in 1946, and by 1949 she left the teaching profession to become a staff writer and editor for *Reveille*, a weekly tabloid newspaper. 'A Christmas Meeting' was her first story to be published in book form, appearing in Cynthia Asquith's *The Second Ghost Book* in 1952. In 1983, Roald Dahl selected this and another of her stories ('Harry') to appear in his own ghost story anthology, where she was one of only two authors to be included twice (the other was A. M. Burrage). She was extremely prolific, publishing over 60 novels, hundreds of short stories, feature articles and radio and television scripts. After Cynthia Asquith's death she also edited several volumes of the *Ghost Book* series, starting with *The Fifth Ghost Book* in 1959.

I have never spent Christmas alone before.

It gives me an uncanny feeling, sitting alone in my 'furnished room,' with my head full of ghosts, and the room full of voices of the past. It's a drowning feeling—all the Christmases of the past coming back in a mad jumble: the childish Christmas, with a house full of relations, a tree in the window, sixpences in the pudding, and the delicious, crinkly stocking in the dark morning; the adolescent Christmas, with mother and father, the War and the bitter cold, and the letters from abroad; the first really grown-up Christmas, with a lover—the snow and the enchantment, red wine and kisses, and the walk in the dark before midnight, with the grounds so white, and the stars diamond bright in a black sky—so many Christmases through the years.

And, now, the first Christmas alone.

But not quite loneliness. A feeling of companionship with all the other people who are spending Christmas alone—millions of them—past and present. A feeling that, if I close my eyes, there will be no past or future, only an endless present which *is* time, because it is all we ever have.

Yes, however cynical you are, however irreligious, it makes you feel queer to be alone at Christmas time.

So I'm absurdly relieved when the young man walks in.

There's nothing romantic about it—I'm a woman of nearly fifty, a spinster schoolma'am with grim, dark hair, and myopic eyes that once were beautiful, and he's a kid of twenty, rather unconventionally dressed with a flowing, wine-coloured tie and black velvet jacket, and brown curls which could do with a taste of the barber's scissors. The effeminacy of his dress is belied by his features—narrow, piercing, blue eyes, and arrogant, jutting nose and chin. Not that he looks strong. The skin is fine-drawn over the prominent features, and he is very white.

He bursts in without knocking, then pauses, says: 'I'm so sorry. I thought this was my room.' He begins to go out, then hesitates and says: 'Are you alone?'

'Yes.'

'It's—queer, being alone at Christmas, isn't it? May I stay and talk?'

'I'd be glad if you would.'

He comes right in, and sits down by the fire.

'I hope you don't think I came in here on purpose, I really did think it was my room,' he explains.

'I'm glad you made the mistake. But you're a very young person to be alone at Christmas time.'

'I wouldn't go back to the country to my family. It would hold up my work. I'm a writer.'

'I see.' I can't help smiling a little. That explains his rather unusual dress. And he takes himself so seriously, this young man! 'Of course, you mustn't waste a precious moment of writing,' I say with a twinkle.

'No, not a moment! That's what my family won't see. They don't appreciate urgency.'

'Families are never appreciative of the artistic nature.'

'No, they aren't,' he agrees seriously.

'What are you writing?'

'Poetry and a diary combined. It's called *My Poems and I*, by Francis Randel. That's my name. My family say there's no point in my writing, that I'm too young. But I don't feel young. Sometimes I feel like an old man, with too much to do before he dies.'

'Revolving faster and faster on the wheel of creativeness.'

'Yes! Yes, exactly! You understand! You must read my work some time. Please read my work! Read my work!' A note of desperation in his voice, a look of fear in his eyes, makes me say:

'We're both getting much too solemn for Christmas Day. I'm going to make you some coffee. And I have a plum cake.'

I move about, clattering cups, spooning coffee into my percolator. But I must have offended him, for, when I look round, I find he has left me. I am absurdly disappointed.

I finish making coffee, however, then turn to the bookshelf in the room. It is piled high with volumes, for which the landlady has apologised profusely: 'Hope you don't mind the books, Miss, but my husband won't part with them, and there's nowhere else to put them. We charge a bit less for the room for that reason.'

'I don't mind,' I said. 'Books are good friends.'

But these aren't very friendly-looking books. I take one at random. Or does some strange fate guide my hand?

Sipping my coffee, inhaling my cigarette smoke, I begin to read the battered little book, published, I see, in Spring, 1852. It's mainly poetry—immature stuff, but vivid. Then there's a kind of diary. More realistic, less affected. Out of curiosity, to see if there are any amusing comparisons, I turn to the entry for Christmas Day, 1851. I read:

'My first Christmas Day alone. I had rather an odd experience. When I went back to my lodgings after a walk, there was a middle-aged woman in my room. I thought, at first, I'd walked into the wrong room, but this was not so, and later, after a pleasant talk, she—disappeared. I suppose she was a ghost. But I wasn't frightened. I liked her. But I do not feel well tonight. Not at all well. I have never felt ill at Christmas before.'

A publisher's note followed the last entry:

FRANCIS RANDEL DIED FROM A SUDDEN HEART ATTACK ON THE NIGHT OF CHRISTMAS DAY, 1851. THE WOMAN MENTIONED IN THIS FINAL ENTRY IN HIS DIARY WAS THE LAST PERSON TO SEE HIM ALIVE. IN SPITE OF REQUESTS FOR HER TO COME FORWARD, SHE NEVER DID SO. HER IDENTITY REMAINS A MYSTERY.

SOMEONE IN THE LIFT

L. P. Hartley

FIRST PUBLISHED IN *THE THIRD GHOST
BOOK* (ED. CYNTHIA ASQUITH, 1955)

Leslie Poles Hartley (1895–1972) started his literary career as a book reviewer, before having a first short story collection published in 1924 and later moving on to novel writing. His most famous book is probably *The Go-Between* (1953), generally regarded as a modern classic. He was a close friend of Cynthia Asquith, and she supported him by including his work in several of her edited collections; 'Someone in the Lift' appeared in *The Third Ghost Book* in 1955. The story includes one of the recurring themes of Hartley's works, a scenario in which comfortable ordinariness becomes a source of horror.

'There's someone coming down in the lift, Mummy!'

'No, my darling, you're wrong, there isn't.'

'But I can see him through the bars—a tall gentleman.'

'You think you can, but it's only a shadow. Now, you'll see, the lift's empty.'

And it always was.

This piece of dialogue, or variations of it, had been repeated at intervals ever since Mr. and Mrs. Maldon and their son Peter had arrived at the Brompton Court Hotel, where, owing to a domestic crisis, they were going to spend Christmas. New to hotel life, the little boy had never seen a lift before and he was fascinated by it. When either of his parents pressed the button to summon it he would take up his stand some distance away to watch it coming down.

The ground floor had a high ceiling, so the lift was visible for some seconds before it touched floor level: and it was then, at its first appearance, that Peter saw the figure. It was always in the same place, facing him in the left-hand corner. He couldn't see it plainly, of course, because of the double grille, the gate of the lift and the gate of the lift-shaft, both of which had to be firmly closed before the lift would work.

He had been told not to use the lift by himself—an unnecessary warning, because he connected the lift with the things that grown-up people did, and unlike most small boys he wasn't over-anxious to share the privileges of his elders: he was content to wonder and admire. The lift appealed to him more as magic than as mechanism. Acceptance of magic made it possible for him to believe that the lift had an occupant when he first saw it, in spite of the demonstrable fact that when it came to rest, giving its fascinating click of finality, the occupant had disappeared.

'If you don't believe me, ask Daddy,' his mother said.

Peter didn't want to do this, and for two reasons, one of which was easier to explain than the other.

'Daddy would say I was being silly,' he said.

'Oh, no, he wouldn't; he never says you're silly.'

This was not quite true. Like all well-regulated modern fathers, Mr. Maldon was aware of the danger of offending a son of tender years: the psychological results might be regrettable. But Freud or no Freud, fathers are still fathers, and sometimes when Peter irritated him Mr. Maldon would let fly. Although he was fond of him, Peter's private vision of his father was of someone more authoritative and awe-inspiring than a stranger, seeing them together, would have guessed.

The other reason, which Peter didn't divulge, was more fantastic. He hadn't asked his father because, when his father was with him, he couldn't see the figure in the lift.

Mrs. Maldon remembered the conversation and told her husband of it. 'The lift's in a dark place,' she said, 'and I dare say he does see something, he's so much nearer to the ground than we are. The bars may cast a shadow and make a sort of pattern that we can't see. I don't know if it's frightening him, but you might have a word with him about it.'

At first Peter was more interested than frightened. Then he began to evolve a theory. If the figure only appeared in his father's absence, didn't it follow that the figure might be, could be, must be, his own father? In what region of his consciousness Peter believed this it would be hard to say; but for imaginative purposes he did believe it and the figure became for him 'Daddy in the lift'. The thought of Daddy in the lift did frighten him, and the neighbourhood of the lift-shaft, in which he felt compelled to hang about, became a place of dread.

Christmas Day was drawing near and the hotel began to deck itself with evergreens. Suspended at the foot of the staircase, in front of the lift, was a bunch of mistletoe, and it was this that gave Mr. Maldon his idea.

As they were standing under it, waiting for the lift, he said to Peter:

'Your mother tells me you've seen someone in the lift who isn't there.'

His voice sounded more accusing than he meant it to, and Peter shrank.

'Oh, not now,' he said, truthfully enough. 'Only sometimes.'

'Your mother told me that you always saw it,' his father said, again more sternly than he meant to. 'And do you know who I think it may be?'

Caught by a gust of terror Peter cried, 'Oh please don't tell me!'

'Why, you silly boy,' said his father reasonably. 'Don't you want to know?'

Ashamed of his cowardice, Peter said he did.

'Why, it's Father Christmas, of course!'

Relief surged through Peter.

'But doesn't Father Christmas come down the chimney?' he asked.

'That was in the old days. He doesn't now. Now he takes the lift!'

Peter thought a moment.

'Will you dress up as Father Christmas this year,' he asked, 'even though it's an hotel?'

'I might.'

'And come down in the lift?'

'Why yes, that's what it's for.'

After this Peter felt happier about the shadowy passenger behind the bars. Father Christmas couldn't hurt anyone, even if he was (as Peter now believed him to be) his own father. Peter was only six but he could remember two Christmas Eves when his father had dressed up as Santa Claus and given him a delicious thrill. He could hardly wait for this one, when the apparition in the corner would at last become a reality.

Alas, two days before Christmas Day the lift broke down. On every floor it served, and there were five (six counting the basement), the forbidding notice 'Out of Order' dangled from the door-handle. Peter complained as loudly as anyone, though secretly, he couldn't have told why, he was glad that the lift no longer functioned; and he didn't mind climbing the four flights to his room, which opened out of his parents' room but had its own door too. By using the stairs he met the workmen (he never knew on which floor they would be) and from them gleaned the latest news about the lift-crisis. They were working overtime, they told him, and were just as anxious as he to see the last of the job. Sometimes they even told each other to put a jerk into it. Always Peter asked them when they would be finished, and they always answered, 'Christmas Eve at latest.'

Peter didn't doubt this. To him the workmen were infallible, possessed of magic powers capable of suspending the ordinary laws that governed lifts. Look how they left the gates open, and shouted to each other up and down the awesome lift-shaft, paying as little attention to the other hotel visitors as if they didn't exist! Only to Peter did they vouchsafe a word.

But Christmas Eve came, the morning passed, the afternoon passed, and still the lift didn't go. The men were working with set faces and a controlled hurry in their movements; they didn't even return Peter's 'Good night' when he passed them on his way to bed. Bed! He had begged to be allowed to stay up this once for dinner; he knew he wouldn't go to sleep, he said, till Father Christmas came. He lay awake, listening to the urgent voices of the men, wondering if each hammer stroke would be the last; and then, just as the clamour was subsiding, he dropped off.

Dreaming, he felt adrift in time. Could it be midnight? No, because his parents had after all consented to his going down to dinner. Now was the time. Averting his eyes from the forbidden lift he stole downstairs. There was a clock in the hall, but it had stopped. In the dining-room there was another clock; but dared he go into the dining-room alone, with no one to guide him and everybody looking at him?

He ventured in, and there, at their table, which he couldn't always pick out, he saw his mother. She saw him, too, and came towards him, threading her way between the tables as if they were just bits of furniture, not alien islands under hostile sway.

'Darling,' she said, 'I couldn't find you—nobody could, but here you are!' She led him back and they sat down. 'Daddy will be with us in a minute.' The minutes passed; suddenly there was a crash. It seemed to come from within, from the kitchen, perhaps. Smiles lit up the faces of the diners. A man at a near-by table laughed and said, 'Something's on the floor! Somebody'll be for it!' 'What is it?' whispered Peter, too excited to speak out loud. 'Is anyone hurt?' 'Oh no, darling, somebody's dropped a tray, that's all.'

To Peter it seemed an anti-climax, this paltry accident that had stolen the thunder of his father's entry, for he didn't doubt that his father would come in as Father Christmas. The suspense was unbearable. 'Can I go into the hall and wait for him?' His mother hesitated and then said yes.

The hall was deserted, even the porter was off duty. Would it be fair, Peter wondered, or would it be cheating and doing himself out of a surprise, if he waited for Father Christmas by the lift? Magic has its rules which mustn't be disobeyed. But he was there now, at his old place in front of the lift; and the lift would come down if he pressed the button.

He knew he mustn't, that it was forbidden, that his father would be angry if he did; yet he reached up and pressed it.

But nothing happened, the lift didn't come, and why? Because some careless person had forgotten to shut the gates— 'monkeying with the lift', his father called it. Perhaps the work-men had forgotten, in their hurry to get home. There was only one thing to do—find out on which floor the gates had been left open, and then shut them.

On their own floor it was, and in his dream it didn't seem strange to Peter that the lift wasn't there, blocking the black hole of the lift-shaft, though he daren't look down it. The gates clicked to. Triumph possessed him, triumph lent him wings; he was back on the ground floor, with his finger on the button. A thrill of power such as he had never known ran through him when the machinery answered to his touch.

But what was this? The lift was coming up from below, not down from above, and there was something wrong with its roof—a jagged hole that let the light through. But the figure was there in its accustomed corner, and this time it hadn't disappeared, it was still there, he could see it through the mazy criss-cross of the bars, a figure in a red robe with white edges, and wearing a red cowl on its head: his father, Father Christmas, Daddy in the lift. But why didn't he look at Peter, and why was his white beard streaked with red?

The two grilles folded back when Peter pushed them. Toys were lying at his father's feet, but he couldn't touch them for they too were red, red and wet as the floor of the lift, red as the jag of lightning that tore through his brain...

TOLD AFTER SUPPER

Jerome K. Jerome

PUBLISHED AS A NOVELETTE, 1891

Jerome Clapp Jerome (1859–1927) was born in Walsall into a middle class family. He later changed his middle name to Klapka, apparently after the Hungarian general György Klapka. The family was not wealthy and Jerome worked in various jobs including as an actor, teacher and clerk, before settling as a journalist for a number of years. He co-founded the satirical magazine *The Idler*, which regularly included supernatural stories, including by authors such as W. W. Jacobs and Eden Philpotts. He is best remembered as the author of the comic masterpiece *Three Men in a Boat* (1889), but he also wrote a number of ghost stories, ranging in tone from comedic to sombrely religious. *Told After Supper*, included in its entirety here, is a linked series of tales which parody the Christmas ghost tradition begun by Charles Dickens in *A Christmas Carol*.

I t was Christmas Eve.

  I begin this way because it is the proper, orthodox, respectable way to begin, and I have been brought up in a proper, orthodox, respectable way, and taught to always do the proper, orthodox, respectable thing; and the habit clings to me.

Of course, as a mere matter of information it is quite unnecessary to mention the date at all. The experienced reader knows it was Christmas Eve, without my telling him. It always is Christmas Eve, in a ghost story.

Christmas Eve is the ghosts' great gala night. On Christmas Eve they hold their annual fete. On Christmas Eve everybody in Ghostland who IS anybody—or rather, speaking of ghosts, one should say, I suppose, every nobody who IS any nobody—comes out to show himself or herself, to see and to be seen, to promenade about and display their winding-sheets and graveclothes to each other, to criticise one another's style, and sneer at one another's complexion.

'Christmas Eve parade,' as I expect they themselves term it, is a function, doubtless, eagerly prepared for and looked forward to throughout Ghostland, especially the swagger set, such as the murdered Barons, the crime-stained Countesses, and the Earls who came over with the Conqueror, and assassinated their relatives, and died raving mad.

Hollow moans and fiendish grins are, one may be sure, energetically practised up. Blood-curdling shrieks and marrow-freezing gestures are probably rehearsed for weeks beforehand. Rusty chains and gory daggers are over-hauled, and put into good working order; and sheets and shrouds, laid carefully by from the previous year's show, are taken down and shaken out, and mended, and aired.

Oh, it is a stirring night in Ghostland, the night of December the twenty-fourth!

Ghosts never come out on Christmas night itself, you may have noticed. Christmas Eve, we suspect, has been too much for them; they are not used to excitement. For about a week after Christmas Eve, the gentlemen ghosts, no doubt, feel as if they were all head, and go about making solemn resolutions to themselves that they will stop in next Christmas Eve; while lady spectres are contradictory and snappish, and liable to burst into tears and leave the room hurriedly on being spoken to, for no perceptible cause whatever.

Ghosts with no position to maintain—mere middle-class ghosts—occasionally, I believe, do a little haunting on off-nights: on All-hallows Eve, and at Midsummer; and some will even run up for a mere local event—to celebrate, for instance, the anniversary of the hanging of somebody's grandfather, or to prophesy a misfortune.

He does love prophesying a misfortune, does the average British ghost. Send him out to prognosticate trouble to some-body, and he is happy. Let him force his way into a peaceful home, and turn the whole house upside down by foretelling a funeral, or predicting a bankruptcy, or hinting at a coming disgrace, or some other terrible disaster, about which nobody in their senses would want to know sooner than they could possibly help, and the prior knowledge of which can serve no useful purpose whatsoever, and he feels that he is combining duty with pleasure. He would never forgive himself if anybody in his family had a trouble and he had not been there for a couple of months beforehand, doing silly tricks on the lawn, or balancing himself on somebody's bed-rail.

Then there are, besides, the very young, or very conscientious ghosts with a lost will or an undiscovered number weighing heavy on their minds, who will haunt steadily all the year round; and also the fussy ghost, who is indignant at having been buried in the dust-bin or in the village pond, and who never gives the parish a single night's quiet until somebody has paid for a first-class funeral for him.

But these are the exceptions. As I have said, the average orthodox ghost does his one turn a year, on Christmas Eve, and is satisfied.

Why on Christmas Eve, of all nights in the year, I never could myself understand. It is invariably one of the most dismal of nights to be out in—cold, muddy, and wet. And besides, at Christmas time, everybody has quite enough to put up with in the way of a houseful of living relations, without wanting the ghosts of any dead ones mooning about the place, I am sure.

There must be something ghostly in the air of Christmas— something about the close, muggy atmosphere that draws up the ghosts, like the dampness of the summer rains brings out the frogs and snails.

And not only do the ghosts themselves always walk on Christmas Eve, but live people always sit and talk about them on Christmas Eve. Whenever five or six English-speaking people meet round a fire on Christmas Eve, they start telling each other ghost stories. Nothing satisfies us on Christmas Eve but to hear each other tell authentic anecdotes about spectres. It is a genial, festive season, and we love to muse upon graves, and dead bodies, and murders, and blood.

There is a good deal of similarity about our ghostly experiences; but this of course is not our fault but the fault of ghosts, who never will try any new performances, but always will keep steadily to old, safe business. The consequence is that, when you have been at one Christmas Eve party, and heard six people relate their adventures with spirits, you do not require to hear any more ghost stories. To listen to any further ghost stories after that would be like sitting out two farcical comedies, or taking in two comic journals; the repetition would become wearisome.

There is always the young man who was, one year, spending the Christmas at a country house, and, on Christmas Eve, they put him to sleep in the west wing. Then in the middle of the night, the room door quietly opens and somebody—generally a lady in her night-dress—walks slowly in, and comes and sits on the bed. The young man thinks it must be one of the visitors, or some relative of the family, though he does not remember having previously seen her, who, unable to go to sleep, and feeling lonesome, all by herself, has come into his room for a chat. He has no idea it is a ghost: he is so unsuspicious. She does not speak, however; and, when he looks again, she is gone!

The young man relates the circumstance at the breakfast-table next morning, and asks each of the ladies present if it were she who was his visitor. But they all assure him that it was not, and the host, who has grown deadly pale, begs him to say no more about the matter, which strikes the young man as a singularly strange request.

After breakfast the host takes the young man into a corner, and explains to him that what he saw was the ghost of a lady who had been murdered in that very bed, or who had murdered somebody else there—it does not really matter which: you can be a ghost by murdering somebody else or by being murdered yourself, whichever you prefer. The murdered ghost is, perhaps, the more popular; but, on the other hand, you can frighten people better if you are the murdered one, because then you can show your wounds and do groans.

Then there is the sceptical guest—it is always 'the guest' who gets let in for this sort of thing, by-the-bye. A ghost never thinks much of his own family: it is 'the guest' he likes to haunt who after listening to the host's ghost story, on Christmas Eve, laughs at it, and says that he does not believe there are such things as ghosts at all; and that he will sleep in the haunted chamber that very night, if they will let him.

Everybody urges him not to be reckless, but he persists in his foolhardiness, and goes up to the Yellow Chamber (or whatever colour the haunted room may be) with a light heart and a candle, and wishes them all good-night, and shuts the door.

Next morning he has got snow-white hair.

He does not tell anybody what he has seen: it is too awful.

There is also the plucky guest, who sees a ghost, and knows it is a ghost, and watches it, as it comes into the room and disappears through the wainscot, after which, as the ghost does not seem to be coming back, and there is nothing, consequently, to be gained by stopping awake, he goes to sleep.

He does not mention having seen the ghost to anybody, for fear of frightening them—some people are so nervous about ghosts,—but determines to wait for the next night, and see if the apparition appears again.

It does appear again, and, this time, he gets out of bed, dresses himself and does his hair, and follows it; and then discovers a secret passage leading from the bedroom down into the beer-cellar,—a passage which, no doubt, was not unfrequently made use of in the bad old days of yore.

After him comes the young man who woke up with a strange sensation in the middle of the night, and found his rich bachelor uncle standing by his bedside. The rich uncle smiled a weird sort of smile and vanished. The young man immediately got up and looked at his watch. It had stopped at half-past four, he having forgotten to wind it.

He made inquiries the next day, and found that, strangely enough, his rich uncle, whose only nephew he was, had married a widow with eleven children at exactly a quarter to twelve, only two days ago.

The young man does not attempt to explain the circumstance. All he does is to vouch for the truth of his narrative.

And, to mention another case, there is the gentleman who is returning home late at night, from a Freemasons' dinner, and who, noticing a light issuing from a ruined abbey, creeps up, and looks through the keyhole. He sees the ghost of a 'grey sister' kissing the ghost of a brown monk, and is so inexpressibly shocked and frightened that he faints on the spot, and is discovered there the next morning, lying in a heap against the door, still speechless, and with his faithful latch-key clasped tightly in his hand.

All these things happen on Christmas Eve, they are all told of on Christmas Eve. For ghost stories to be told on any other evening than the evening of the twenty-fourth of December would be impossible in English society as at present regulated. Therefore, in introducing the sad but authentic ghost stories that follow hereafter, I feel that it is unnecessary to inform the student of Anglo-Saxon literature that the date on which they were told and on which the incidents took place was—Christmas Eve.

Nevertheless, I do so.

HOW THE STORIES CAME TO BE TOLD

It was Christmas Eve! Christmas Eve at my Uncle John's; Christmas Eve (There is too much 'Christmas Eve' about this book. I can see that myself. It is beginning to get monotonous even to me. But I don't see how to avoid it now.) at No. 47 Laburnham Grove, Tooting! Christmas Eve in the dimly-lighted (there was a gas-strike on) front parlour, where the flickering firelight threw strange shadows on the highly coloured wall-paper, while without, in the wild street, the storm raged pitilessly, and the wind, like some unquiet spirit, flew, moaning, across the square, and passed, wailing with a troubled cry, round by the milk-shop.

We had had supper, and were sitting round, talking and smoking.

We had had a very good supper—a very good supper, indeed. Unpleasantness has occurred since, in our family, in connection with this party. Rumours have been put about in our family, concerning the matter generally, but more particularly concerning my own share in it, and remarks have been passed which have not so much surprised me, because I know what our family are, but which have pained me very much. As for my Aunt Maria, I do not know when I shall care to see her again. I should have thought Aunt Maria might have known me better.

But although injustice—gross injustice, as I shall explain later on—has been done to myself, that shall not deter me from doing justice to others; even to those who have made unfeeling insinuations. I will do justice to Aunt Maria's hot veal pasties, and toasted lobsters, followed by her own special make of cheesecakes, warm (there is no sense, to my thinking, in cold cheesecakes; you lose half the flavour), and washed down by Uncle John's own particular old ale, and acknowledge that they were most tasty. I did justice to them then; Aunt Maria herself could not but admit that.

After supper, Uncle brewed some whisky-punch. I did justice to that also; Uncle John himself said so. He said he was glad to notice that I liked it.

Aunt went to bed soon after supper, leaving the local curate, old Dr. Scrubbles, Mr. Samuel Coombes, our member of the County Council, Teddy Biffles, and myself to keep Uncle company. We agreed that it was too early to give in for some time yet, so Uncle brewed another bowl of punch; and I think we all did justice to that—at least I know I did. It is a passion with me, is the desire to do justice.

We sat up for a long while, and the Doctor brewed some gin-punch later on, for a change, though I could not taste much difference myself. But it was all good, and we were very happy—everybody was so kind.

Uncle John told us a very funny story in the course of the evening. Oh, it WAS a funny story! I forget what it was about now, but I know it amused me very much at the time; I do not think I ever laughed so much in all my life. It is strange that I cannot recollect that story too, because he told it us four times. And it was entirely our own fault that he did not tell it us a fifth. After that, the Doctor sang a very clever song, in the course of which he imitated all the different animals in a farmyard. He did mix them a bit. He brayed for the bantam cock, and crowed for the pig; but we knew what he meant all right.

I started relating a most interesting anecdote, but was somewhat surprised to observe, as I went on, that nobody was paying the slightest attention to me whatever. I thought this rather rude of them at first, until it dawned upon me that I was talking to myself all the time, instead of out aloud, so that, of course, they did not know that I was telling them a tale at all, and were probably puzzled to understand the meaning of my animated expression and eloquent gestures. It was a most curious mistake for any one to make. I never knew such a thing happen to me before.

Later on, our curate did tricks with cards. He asked us if we had ever seen a game called the 'Three Card Trick.' He said it was an artifice by means of which low, unscrupulous men, frequenters of race-meetings and such like haunts, swindled foolish young fellows out of their money. He said it was a very simple trick to do: it all depended on the quickness of the hand. It was the quickness of the hand deceived the eye.

He said he would show us the imposture so that we might be warned against it, and not be taken in by it; and he fetched Uncle's pack of cards from the tea-caddy, and, selecting three cards from the pack, two plain cards and one picture card, sat down on the hearthrug, and explained to us what he was going to do.

He said: 'Now I shall take these three cards in my hand—so—and let you all see them. And then I shall quietly lay them down on the rug, with the backs uppermost, and ask you to pick out the picture card. And you'll think you know which one it is.' And he did it.

Old Mr. Coombes, who is also one of our churchwardens, said it was the middle card.

'You fancy you saw it,' said our curate, smiling.

'I don't "fancy" anything at all about it,' replied Mr. Coombes, 'I tell you it's the middle card. I'll bet you half a dollar it's the middle card.'

'There you are, that's just what I was explaining to you,' said our curate, turning to the rest of us; 'that's the way these foolish young fellows that I was speaking of are lured on to lose their money. They make sure they know the card, they fancy they saw it. They don't grasp the idea that it is the quickness of the hand that has deceived their eye.'

He said he had known young men go off to a boat race, or a cricket match, with pounds in their pocket, and come home, early in the afternoon, stone broke; having lost all their money at this demoralising game.

He said he should take Mr. Coombes's half-crown, because it would teach Mr. Coombes a very useful lesson, and probably be the means of saving Mr. Coombes's money in the future; and he should give the two-and-sixpence to the blanket fund.

'Don't you worry about that,' retorted old Mr. Coombes. 'Don't you take the half-crown *out* of the blanket fund: that's all.'

And he put his money on the middle card, and turned it up. Sure enough, it really was the queen!

We were all very much surprised, especially the curate.

He said that it did sometimes happen that way, though—that a man did sometimes lay on the right card, by accident.

Our curate said it was, however, the most unfortunate thing a man could do for himself, if he only knew it, because, when a man tried and won, it gave him a taste for the so-called sport, and it lured him on into risking again and again; until he had to retire from the contest, a broken and ruined man.

Then he did the trick again. Mr. Coombes said it was the card next the coal-scuttle this time, and wanted to put five shillings on it.

We laughed at him, and tried to persuade him against it. He would listen to no advice, however, but insisted on plunging.

Our curate said very well then: he had warned him, and that was all that he could do. If he (Mr. Coombes) was determined to make a fool of himself, he (Mr. Coombes) must do so.

Our curate said he should take the five shillings and that would put things right again with the blanket fund.

So Mr. Coombes put two half-crowns on the card next the coal-scuttle and turned it up.

Sure enough, it was the queen again!

After that, Uncle John had a florin on, and *he* won.

And then we all played at it; and we all won. All except the curate, that is. He had a very bad quarter of an hour. I never knew a man have such hard luck at cards. He lost every time.

We had some more punch after that; and Uncle made such a funny mistake in brewing it: he left out the whisky. Oh, we did laugh at him, and we made him put in double quantity afterwards, as a forfeit.

Oh, we did have such fun that evening!

And then, somehow or other, we must have got on to ghosts; because the next recollection I have is that we were telling ghost stories to each other.

TEDDY BIFFLES' STORY

Teddy Biffles told the first story, I will let him repeat it here in his own words.

(Do not ask me how it is that I recollect his own exact words—whether I took them down in shorthand at the time, or whether he had the story written out, and handed me the MS. afterwards for publication in this book, because I should not tell you if you did. It is a trade secret.)

Biffles called his story—

Johnson and Emily
or
The Faithful Ghost

(TEDDY BIFFLES' STORY)

I was little more than a lad when I first met with Johnson. I was home for the Christmas holidays, and, it being Christmas Eve, I had been allowed to sit up very late. On opening the door of my little bedroom, to go in, I found myself face to face with Johnson, who was coming out. It passed through me, and uttering a long low wail of misery, disappeared out of the staircase window.

I was startled for the moment—I was only a schoolboy at the time, and had never seen a ghost before,—and felt a little nervous about going to bed. But, on reflection, I remembered that it was only sinful people that spirits could do any harm to, and so tucked myself up, and went to sleep.

In the morning I told the Pater what I had seen.

'Oh yes, that was old Johnson,' he answered. 'Don't you be frightened of that; he lives here.' And then he told me the poor thing's history.

It seemed that Johnson, when it was alive, had loved, in early life, the daughter of a former lessee of our house, a very beautiful girl, whose Christian name had been Emily. Father did not know her other name.

Johnson was too poor to marry the girl, so he kissed her good-bye, told her he would soon be back, and went off to Australia to make his fortune.

But Australia was not then what it became later on. Travellers through the bush were few and far between in those early days; and, even when one was caught, the portable property found upon the body was often of hardly sufficiently negotiable value to pay the simple funeral expenses rendered necessary. So that it took Johnson nearly twenty years to make his fortune.

The self-imposed task was accomplished at last, however, and then, having successfully eluded the police, and got clear out of the Colony, he returned to England, full of hope and joy, to claim his bride.

He reached the house to find it silent and deserted. All that the neighbours could tell him was that, soon after his own departure, the family had, on one foggy night, unostentatiously disappeared, and that nobody had ever seen or heard anything of them since, although the landlord and most of the local tradesmen had made searching inquiries.

Poor Johnson, frenzied with grief, sought his lost love all over the world. But he never found her, and, after years of fruitless effort, he returned to end his lonely life in the very house where, in the happy bygone days, he and his beloved Emily had passed so many blissful hours.

He had lived there quite alone, wandering about the empty rooms, weeping and calling to his Emily to come back to him; and when the poor old fellow died, his ghost still kept the business on.

It was there, the Pater said, when he took the house, and the agent had knocked ten pounds a year off the rent in consequence.

After that, I was continually meeting Johnson about the place at all times of the night, and so, indeed, were we all. We used to walk round it and stand aside to let it pass, at first; but, when we grew at home with it, and there seemed no necessity for so much ceremony, we used to walk straight through it. You could not say it was ever much in the way.

It was a gentle, harmless, old ghost, too, and we all felt very sorry for it, and pitied it. The women folk, indeed, made quite a pet of it, for a while. Its faithfulness touched them so.

But as time went on, it grew to be a bit of a bore. You see it was full of sadness. There was nothing cheerful or genial about it. You felt sorry for it, but it irritated you. It would sit on the stairs and cry for hours at a stretch; and, whenever we woke up in the night, one was sure to hear it pottering about the passages and in and out of the different rooms, moaning and sighing, so that we could not get to sleep again very easily. And when we had a party on, it would come and sit outside the drawing-room door, and sob all the time. It did not do anybody any harm exactly, but it cast a gloom over the whole affair.

'Oh, I'm getting sick of this old fool,' said the Pater, one evening (the Dad can be very blunt, when he is put out, as you know), after Johnson had been more of a nuisance than usual, and had spoiled a good game of whist, by sitting up the chimney and groaning, till nobody knew what were trumps or what suit had been led, even. 'We shall have to get rid of him, somehow or other. I wish I knew how to do it.'

'Well,' said the Mater, 'depend upon it, you'll never see the last of him until he's found Emily's grave. That's what he is after. You find Emily's grave, and put him on to that, and he'll stop there. That's the only thing to do. You mark my words.'

The idea seemed reasonable, but the difficulty in the way was that we none of us knew where Emily's grave was any more than the ghost of Johnson himself did. The Governor suggested palming off some other Emily's grave upon the poor thing, but, as luck would have it, there did not seem to have been an Emily of any sort buried anywhere for miles round. I never came across a neighbourhood so utterly destitute of dead Emilies.

I thought for a bit, and then I hazarded a suggestion myself.

'Couldn't we fake up something for the old chap?' I queried. 'He seems a simple-minded old sort. He might take it in. Anyhow, we could but try.'

'By Jove, so we will,' exclaimed my father; and the very next morning we had the workmen in, and fixed up a little mound at the bottom of the orchard with a tombstone over it, bearing the following inscription:

SACRED TO THE MEMORY OF EMILY

HER LAST WORDS WERE—'TELL JOHNSON I LOVE HIM'

'That ought to fetch him,' mused the Dad as he surveyed the work when finished. 'I am sure I hope it does.'

It did!

We lured him down there that very night; and—well, there, it was one of the most pathetic things I have ever seen, the way Johnson sprang upon that tombstone and wept. Dad and old Squibbins, the gardener, cried like children when they saw it.

Johnson has never troubled us any more in the house since then. It spends every night now, sobbing on the grave, and seems quite happy.

'There still?' Oh yes. I'll take you fellows down and show you it, next time you come to our place: 10 p.m. to 4 a.m. are its general hours, 10 to 2 on Saturdays.

INTERLUDE—THE DOCTOR'S STORY

It made me cry very much, that story, young Biffles told it with so much feeling. We were all a little thoughtful after it, and I noticed even the old Doctor covertly wipe away a tear. Uncle John brewed another bowl of punch, however, and we gradually grew more resigned.

The Doctor, indeed, after a while became almost cheerful, and told us about the ghost of one of his patients.

I cannot give you his story. I wish I could. They all said afterwards that it was the best of the lot—the most ghastly and terrible—but I could not make any sense of it myself. It seemed so incomplete.

He began all right and then something seemed to happen, and then he was finishing it. I cannot make out what he did with the middle of the story.

It ended up, I know, however, with somebody finding something; and that put Mr. Coombes in mind of a very curious affair that took place at an old Mill, once kept by his brother-in-law.

Mr. Coombes said he would tell us his story, and before anybody could stop him, he had begun.

Mr. Coombes said the story was called—

The Haunted Mill
or
The Ruined Home

(MR. COOMBES'S STORY)

Well, you all know my brother-in-law, Mr. Parkins (began Mr. Coombes, taking the long clay pipe from his mouth, and putting it behind his ear: we did not know his brother-in-law, but we said we did, so as to save time), and you know of course that he once took a lease of an old Mill in Surrey, and went to live there.

Now you must know that, years ago, this very mill had been occupied by a wicked old miser, who died there, leaving—so it was rumoured—all his money hidden somewhere about the place. Naturally enough, every one who had since come to live at the mill had tried to find the treasure; but none had ever succeeded, and the local wiseacres said that nobody ever would, unless the ghost of the miserly miller should, one day, take a fancy to one of the tenants, and disclose to him the secret of the hiding-place.

My brother-in-law did not attach much importance to the story, regarding it as an old woman's tale, and, unlike his predecessors, made no attempt whatever to discover the hidden gold.

'Unless business was very different then from what it is now,' said my brother-in-law, 'I don't see how a miller could very well have saved anything, however much of a miser he might have been: at all events, not enough to make it worth the trouble of looking for it.'

Still, he could not altogether get rid of the idea of that treasure.

One night he went to bed. There was nothing very extraordinary about that, I admit. He often did go to bed of a night. What *was* remarkable, however, was that exactly as the clock of the village church chimed the last stroke of twelve, my brother-in-law woke up with a start, and felt himself quite unable to go to sleep again.

Joe (his Christian name was Joe) sat up in bed, and looked around.

At the foot of the bed something stood very still, wrapped in shadow.

It moved into the moonlight, and then my brother-in-law saw that it was the figure of a wizened little old man, in knee-breeches and a pig-tail.

In an instant the story of the hidden treasure and the old miser flashed across his mind.

'He's come to show me where it's hid,' thought my brother-in-law; and he resolved that he would not spend all this money on himself, but would devote a small percentage of it towards doing good to others.

The apparition moved towards the door: my brother-in-law put on his trousers and followed it. The ghost went downstairs into the kitchen, glided over and stood in front of the hearth, sighed and disappeared.

Next morning, Joe had a couple of bricklayers in, and made them haul out the stove and pull down the chimney, while he stood behind with a potato-sack in which to put the gold.

They knocked down half the wall, and never found so much as a four-penny bit. My brother-in-law did not know what to think.

The next night the old man appeared again, and again led the way into the kitchen. This time, however, instead of going to the fireplace, it stood more in the middle of the room, and sighed there.

'Oh, I see what he means now,' said my brother-in-law to himself; 'it's under the floor. Why did the old idiot go and stand up against the stove, so as to make me think it was up the chimney?'

They spent the next day in taking up the kitchen floor; but the only thing they found was a three-pronged fork, and the handle of that was broken.

On the third night, the ghost reappeared, quite unabashed, and for a third time made for the kitchen. Arrived there, it looked up at the ceiling and vanished.

'Umph! he don't seem to have learned much sense where he's been to,' muttered Joe, as he trotted back to bed; 'I should have thought he might have done that at first.'

Still, there seemed no doubt now where the treasure lay, and the first thing after breakfast they started pulling down the ceiling. They got every inch of the ceiling down, and they took up the boards of the room above.

They discovered about as much treasure as you would expect to find in an empty quart-pot.

On the fourth night, when the ghost appeared, as usual, my brother-in-law was so wild that he threw his boots at it; and the boots passed through the body, and broke a looking-glass.

On the fifth night, when Joe awoke, as he always did now at twelve, the ghost was standing in a dejected attitude, looking very miserable. There was an appealing look in its large sad eyes that quite touched my brother-in-law.

'After all,' he thought, 'perhaps the silly chap's doing his best. Maybe he has forgotten where he really did put it, and is trying to remember. I'll give him another chance.'

The ghost appeared grateful and delighted at seeing Joe prepare to follow him, and led the way into the attic, pointed to the ceiling, and vanished.

'Well, he's hit it this time, I do hope,' said my brother-in-law; and next day they set to work to take the roof off the place.

It took them three days to get the roof thoroughly off, and all they found was a bird's nest; after securing which they covered up the house with tarpaulins, to keep it dry.

You might have thought that would have cured the poor fellow of looking for treasure. But it didn't.

He said there must be something in it all, or the ghost would never keep on coming as it did; and that, having gone so far, he would go on to the end, and solve the mystery, cost what it might.

Night after night, he would get out of his bed and follow that spectral old fraud about the house. Each night, the old man would indicate a different place; and, on each following day, my brother-in-law would proceed to break up the mill at the point indicated, and look for the treasure. At the end of three weeks, there was not a room in the mill fit to live in. Every wall had been pulled down, every floor had been taken up, every ceiling had had a hole knocked in it. And then, as suddenly as they had begun, the ghost's visits ceased; and my brother-in-law was left in peace, to rebuild the place at his leisure.

'What induced the old image to play such a silly trick upon a family man and a ratepayer?' Ah! that's just what I cannot tell you.

Some said that the ghost of the wicked old man had done it to punish my brother-in-law for not believing in him at first; while others held that the apparition was probably that of some deceased local plumber and glazier, who would naturally take an interest in seeing a house knocked about and spoilt. But nobody knew anything for certain.

INTERLUDE

We had some more punch, and then the curate told us a story.

I could not make head or tail of the curate's story, so I cannot retail it to you. We none of us could make head or tail of that story. It was a good story enough, so far as material went. There seemed to be an enormous amount of plot, and enough incident to have made a dozen novels. I never before heard a story containing so much incident, nor one dealing with so many varied characters.

I should say that every human being our curate had ever known or met, or heard of, was brought into that story. There were simply hundreds of them. Every five seconds he would introduce into the tale a completely fresh collection of characters accompanied by a brand new set of incidents.

This was the sort of story it was:

'Well, then, my uncle went into the garden, and got his gun, but, of course, it wasn't there, and Scroggins said he didn't believe it.'

'Didn't believe what? Who's Scroggins?'

'Scroggins! Oh, why he was the other man, you know—it was his wife.'

'*What* was his wife—what's *she* got to do with it?'

'Why, that's what I'm telling you. It was she that found the hat. She'd come up with her cousin to London—her cousin was my sister-in-law, and the other niece had married a man named Evans, and Evans, after it was all over, had taken the box round to Mr. Jacobs', because Jacobs' father had seen the man, when he was alive, and when he was dead, Joseph—'

'Now look here, never you mind Evans and the box; what's become of your uncle and the gun?'

'The gun! What gun?'

'Why, the gun that your uncle used to keep in the garden, and that wasn't there. What did he do with it? Did he kill any of these people with it—these Jacobses and Evanses and Scrogginses and Josephses? Because, if so, it was a good and useful work, and we should enjoy hearing about it.'

'No—oh no—how could he?—he had been built up alive in the wall, you know, and when Edward IV spoke to the abbot about it, my sister said that in her then state of health she could not and would not, as it was endangering the child's life. So they christened it Horatio, after her own son, who had been killed at Waterloo before he was born, and Lord Napier himself said—'

'Look here, do you know what you are talking about?' we asked him at this point.

He said 'No,' but he knew it was every word of it true, because his aunt had seen it herself. Whereupon we covered him over with the tablecloth, and he went to sleep.

And then Uncle told us a story.

Uncle said his was a real story.

The Ghost of the Blue Chamber

(MY UNCLE'S STORY)

'I don't want to make you fellows nervous,' began my uncle in a peculiarly impressive, not to say blood-curdling, tone of voice, 'and if you would rather that I did not mention it, I won't; but, as a matter of fact, this very house, in which we are now sitting, is haunted.'

'You don't say that!' exclaimed Mr. Coombes.

'What's the use of your saying I don't say it when I have just said it?' retorted my uncle somewhat pettishly. 'You do talk so foolishly. I tell you the house is haunted. Regularly on Christmas Eve the Blue Chamber [they called the room next to the nursery the 'blue chamber,' at my uncle's, most of the toilet service being of that shade] is haunted by the ghost of a sinful man—a man who once killed a Christmas wait with a lump of coal.'

'How did he do it?' asked Mr. Coombes, with eager anxiousness. 'Was it difficult?'

'I do not know how he did it,' replied my uncle; 'he did not explain the process. The wait had taken up a position just inside the front gate, and was singing a ballad. It is presumed that, when he opened his mouth for B flat, the lump of coal was thrown by the sinful man from one of the windows, and that it went down the wait's throat and choked him.'

'You want to be a good shot, but it is certainly worth trying,' murmured Mr. Coombes thoughtfully.

'But that was not his only crime, alas!' added my uncle. 'Prior to that he had killed a solo cornet-player.'

'No! Is that really a fact?' exclaimed Mr. Coombes.

'Of course it's a fact,' answered my uncle testily; 'at all events, as much a fact as you can expect to get in a case of this sort.

'How very captious you are this evening. The circumstantial evidence was overwhelming. The poor fellow, the cornet-player, had been in the neighbourhood barely a month. Old Mr. Bishop, who kept the 'Jolly Sand Boys' at the time, and from whom I had the story, said he had never known a more hard-working and energetic solo cornet-player. He, the cornet-player, only knew two tunes, but Mr. Bishop said that the man could not have played with more vigour, or for more hours in a day, if he had known forty. The two tunes he did play were 'Annie Laurie' and 'Home, Sweet Home'; and as regarded his performance of the former melody, Mr. Bishop said that a mere child could have told what it was meant for.

'This musician—this poor, friendless artist used to come regularly and play in this street just opposite for two hours every evening. One evening he was seen, evidently in response to an invitation, going into this very house, *but was never seen coming out of it!*'

'Did the townsfolk try offering any reward for his recovery?' asked Mr. Coombes.

'Not a ha'penny,' replied my uncle.

'Another summer,' continued my uncle, 'a German band visited here, intending—so they announced on their arrival—to stay till the autumn.

'On the second day from their arrival, the whole company, as fine and healthy a body of men as one could wish to see, were invited to dinner by this sinful man, and, after spending the whole of the next twenty-four hours in bed, left the town a broken and dyspeptic crew; the parish doctor, who had attended them, giving it as his opinion that it was doubtful if they would, any of them, be fit to play an air again.'

'You—you don't know the recipe, do you?' asked Mr. Coombes.

'Unfortunately I do not,' replied my uncle; 'but the chief ingredient was said to have been railway refreshment-room pork-pie.

'I forget the man's other crimes,' my uncle went on; 'I used to know them all at one time, but my memory is not what it was. I do not, however, believe I am doing his memory an injustice in believing that he was not entirely unconnected with the death, and subsequent burial, of a gentleman who used to play the harp with his toes; and that neither was he altogether unresponsible for the lonely grave of an unknown stranger who had once visited the neighbourhood, an Italian peasant lad, a performer upon the barrel-organ.

'Every Christmas Eve,' said my uncle, cleaving with low impressive tones the strange awed silence that, like a shadow, seemed to have slowly stolen into and settled down upon the room, 'the ghost of this sinful man haunts the Blue Chamber, in this very house. There, from midnight until cock-crow, amid wild muffled shrieks and groans and mocking laughter and the ghostly sound of horrid blows, it does fierce phantom fight with the spirits of the solo cornet-player and the murdered wait, assisted at intervals, by the shades of the German band; while the ghost of the strangled harpist plays mad ghostly melodies with ghostly toes on the ghost of a broken harp.

Uncle said the Blue Chamber was comparatively useless as a sleeping-apartment on Christmas Eve.

'Hark!' said uncle, raising a warning hand towards the ceiling, while we held our breath, and listened; 'Hark! I believe they are at it now—in the *Blue Chamber*!'

THE BLUE CHAMBER

I rose up, and said that I would sleep in the Blue Chamber.

Before I tell you my own story, however—the story of what happened in the Blue Chamber—I would wish to preface it with—

A PERSONAL EXPLANATION

I feel a good deal of hesitation about telling you this story of my own. You see it is not a story like the other stories that I have been telling you, or rather that Teddy Biffles, Mr. Coombes, and my uncle have been telling you: it is a true story. It is not a story told by a person sitting round a fire on Christmas Eve, drinking whisky punch: it is a record of events that actually happened.

Indeed, it is not a 'story' at all, in the commonly accepted meaning of the word: it is a report. It is, I feel, almost out of place in a book of this kind. It is more suitable to a biography, or an English history.

There is another thing that makes it difficult for me to tell you this story, and that is, that it is all about myself. In telling you this story, I shall have to keep on talking about myself; and talking about ourselves is what we modern-day authors have a strong objection to doing. If we literary men of the new school have one praiseworthy yearning more ever present to our minds than another it is the yearning never to appear in the slightest degree egotistical.

I myself, so I am told, carry this coyness—this shrinking reticence concerning anything connected with my own personality, almost too far; and people grumble at me because of it. People come to me and say—

'Well, now, why don't you talk about yourself a bit? That's what we want to read about. Tell us something about yourself.'

But I have always replied, 'No.' It is not that I do not think the subject an interesting one. I cannot myself conceive of any topic more likely to prove fascinating to the world as a whole, or at all events to the cultured portion of it. But I will not do it, on principle. It is inartistic, and it sets a bad example to the younger men. Other writers (a few of them) do it, I know; but I will not—not as a rule.

Under ordinary circumstances, therefore, I should not tell you this story at all. I should say to myself, 'No! It is a good story, it is a moral story, it is a strange, weird, enthralling sort of a story; and the public, I know, would like to hear it; and I should like to tell it to them; but it is all about myself—about what I said, and what I saw, and what I did, and I cannot do it. My retiring, anti-egotistical nature will not permit me to talk in this way about myself.'

But the circumstances surrounding this story are not ordinary, and there are reasons prompting me, in spite of my modesty, to rather welcome the opportunity of relating it.

As I stated at the beginning, there has been unpleasantness in our family over this party of ours, and, as regards myself in particular, and my share in the events I am now about to set forth, gross injustice has been done me.

As a means of replacing my character in its proper light—of dispelling the clouds of calumny and misconception with which it has been darkened, I feel that my best course is to give a simple, dignified narration of the plain facts, and allow the unprejudiced to judge for themselves. My chief object, I candidly confess, is to clear myself from unjust aspersion. Spurred by this motive—and I think it is an honourable and a right motive—I find I am enabled to overcome my usual repugnance to talking about myself, and can thus tell—

MY OWN STORY

As soon as my uncle had finished his story, I, as I have already told you, rose up and said that *I* would sleep in the Blue Chamber that very night.

'Never!' cried my uncle, springing up. 'You shall not put yourself in this deadly peril. Besides, the bed is not made.'

'Never mind the bed,' I replied. 'I have lived in furnished apartments for gentlemen, and have been accustomed to sleep on beds that have never been made from one year's end to the other. Do not thwart me in my resolve. I am young, and have had a clear conscience now for over a month. The spirits will not harm me. I may even do them some little good, and induce them to be quiet and go away. Besides, I should like to see the show.'

Saying which, I sat down again. (How Mr. Coombes came to be in my chair, instead of at the other side of the room, where he had been all the evening; and why he never offered to apologise when I sat right down on top of him; and why young Biffles should have tried to palm himself off upon me as my Uncle John, and induced me, under that erroneous impression, to shake him by the hand for nearly three minutes, and tell him that I had always regarded him as father,—are matters that, to this day, I have never been able to fully understand.)

They tried to dissuade me from what they termed my fool-hardy enterprise, but I remained firm, and claimed my privilege. I was 'the guest.' 'The guest' always sleeps in the haunted chamber on Christmas Eve; it is his perquisite.

They said that if I put it on that footing, they had, of course, no answer; and they lighted a candle for me, and accompanied me upstairs in a body.

Whether elevated by the feeling that I was doing a noble action, or animated by a mere general consciousness of recti-tude, is not for me to say, but I went upstairs that night with remarkable buoyancy. It was as much as I could do to stop at the landing when I came to it; I felt I wanted to go on up to the roof. But, with the help of the banisters, I restrained my ambi-tion, wished them all good-night, and went in and shut the door.

Things began to go wrong with me from the very first. The candle tumbled out of the candlestick before my hand was off the lock. It kept on tumbling out of the candlestick, and every time I picked put it up and put it in, it tumbled out again: I never saw such a slippery candle. I gave up attempting to use the candlestick at last, and carried the candle about in my hand; and, even then, it would not keep upright. So I got wild and threw it out of window, and undressed and went to bed in the dark.

I did not go to sleep,—I did not feel sleepy at all,—I lay on my back, looking up at the ceiling, and thinking of things. I wish I could remember some of the ideas that came to me as I lay there, because they were so amusing. I laughed at them myself till the bed shook.

I had been lying like this for half an hour or so, and had forgotten all about the ghost, when, on casually casting my eyes round the room, I noticed for the first time a singularly contented-looking phantom, sitting in the easy-chair by the fire, smoking the ghost of a long clay pipe.

I fancied for the moment, as most people would under similar circumstances, that I must be dreaming. I sat up, and rubbed my eyes.

No! It was a ghost, clear enough. I could see the back of the chair through his body. He looked over towards me, took the shadowy pipe from his lips, and nodded.

The most surprising part of the whole thing to me was that I did not feel in the least alarmed. If anything, I was rather pleased to see him. It was company.

I said, 'Good evening. It's been a cold day!'

He said he had not noticed it himself, but dared say I was right.

We remained silent for a few seconds, and then, wishing to put it pleasantly, I said, 'I believe I have the honour of addressing the ghost of the gentleman who had the accident with the wait?'

He smiled, and said it was very good of me to remember it. One wait was not much to boast of, but still, every little helped.

I was somewhat staggered at his answer. I had expected a groan of remorse. The ghost appeared, on the contrary, to be rather conceited over the business. I thought that, as he had taken my reference to the wait so quietly, perhaps he would not be offended if I questioned him about the organ-grinder. I felt curious about that poor boy.

'Is it true,' I asked, 'that you had a hand in the death of that Italian peasant lad who came to the town once with a barrel-organ that played nothing but Scotch airs?'

He quite fired up. 'Had a hand in it!' he exclaimed indignantly. 'Who has dared to pretend that he assisted me? I murdered the youth myself. Nobody helped me. Alone I did it. Show me the man who says I didn't.'

I calmed him. I assured him that I had never, in my own mind, doubted that he was the real and only assassin, and I went on and asked him what he had done with the body of the cornet-player he had killed.

He said, 'To which one may you be alluding?'

'Oh, were there any more then?' I inquired.

He smiled, and gave a little cough. He said he did not like to appear to be boasting, but that, counting trombones, there were seven.

'Dear me!' I replied, 'you must have had quite a busy time of it, one way and another.'

He said that perhaps he ought not to be the one to say so, but that really, speaking of ordinary middle-society, he thought there were few ghosts who could look back upon a life of more sustained usefulness.

He puffed away in silence for a few seconds, while I sat watching him. I had never seen a ghost smoking a pipe before, that I could remember, and it interested me.

I asked him what tobacco he used, and he replied, 'The ghost of cut cavendish, as a rule.'

He explained that the ghost of all the tobacco that a man smoked in life belonged to him when he became dead. He said he himself had smoked a good deal of cut cavendish when he was alive, so that he was well supplied with the ghost of it now.

I observed that it was a useful thing to know that, and I made up my mind to smoke as much tobacco as ever I could before I died.

I thought I might as well start at once, so I said I would join him in a pipe, and he said, 'Do, old man'; and I reached over and got out the necessary paraphernalia from my coat pocket and lit up.

We grew quite chummy after that, and he told me all his crimes. He said he had lived next door once to a young lady who was learning to play the guitar, while a gentleman who practised on the bass-viol lived opposite. And he, with fiend-ish cunning, had introduced these two unsuspecting young people to one another, and had persuaded them to elope with each other against their parents' wishes, and take their musical instruments with them; and they had done so, and, before the honeymoon was over, *she* had broken his head with the bass-viol, and *he* had tried to cram the guitar down her throat, and had injured her for life.

My friend said he used to lure muffin-men into the passage and then stuff them with their own wares till they burst and died. He said he had quieted eighteen that way.

Young men and women who recited long and dreary poems at evening parties, and callow youths who walked about the streets late at night, playing concertinas, he used to get together and poison in batches of ten, so as to save expense; and park orators and temperance lecturers he used to shut up six in a small room with a glass of water and a collection-box apiece, and let them talk each other to death.

It did one good to listen to him.

I asked him when he expected the other ghosts—the ghosts of the wait and the cornet-player, and the German band that Uncle John had mentioned. He smiled, and said they would never come again, any of them.

I said, 'Why; isn't it true, then, that they meet you here every Christmas Eve for a row?'

He replied that it *was* true. Every Christmas Eve, for twenty-five years, had he and they fought in that room; but they would never trouble him nor anybody else again. One by one, had he laid them out, spoilt, and utterly useless for all haunting purposes. He had finished off the last German-band ghost that very evening, just before I came upstairs, and had thrown what was left of it out through the slit between the window-sashes. He said it would never be worth calling a ghost again.

'I suppose you will still come yourself, as usual?' I said. 'They would be sorry to miss you, I know.'

'Oh, I don't know,' he replied; 'there's nothing much to come for now. Unless,' he added kindly, '*you* are going to be here. I'll come if you will sleep here next Christmas Eve.

'I have taken a liking to you,' he continued; 'you don't fly off, screeching, when you see a party, and your hair doesn't stand on end. You've no idea,' he said, 'how sick I am of seeing people's hair standing on end.'

He said it irritated him.

Just then a slight noise reached us from the yard below, and he started and turned deathly black.

'You are ill,' I cried, springing towards him; 'tell me the best thing to do for you. Shall I drink some brandy, and give you the ghost of it?'

He remained silent, listening intently for a moment, and then he gave a sigh of relief, and the shade came back to his cheek.

'It's all right,' he murmured; 'I was afraid it was the cock.'

'Oh, it's too early for that,' I said. 'Why, it's only the middle of the night.'

'Oh, that doesn't make any difference to those cursed chickens,' he replied bitterly. 'They would just as soon crow in the middle of the night as at any other time—sooner, if they thought it would spoil a chap's evening out. I believe they do it on purpose.'

He said a friend of his, the ghost of a man who had killed a water-rate collector, used to haunt a house in Long Acre, where they kept fowls in the cellar, and every time a policeman went by and flashed his bull's-eye down the grating, the old cock there would fancy it was the sun, and start crowing like mad; when, of course, the poor ghost had to dissolve, and it would, in consequence, get back home sometimes as early as one o'clock in the morning, swearing fearfully because it had only been out for an hour.

I agreed that it seemed very unfair.

'Oh, it's an absurd arrangement altogether,' he continued, quite angrily. 'I can't imagine what our old man could have been thinking of when he made it. As I have said to him, over and over again, "Have a fixed time, and let everybody stick to it—say four o'clock in summer, and six in winter. Then one would know what one was about."

'How do you manage when there isn't any cock handy?' I inquired.

He was on the point of replying, when again he started and listened. This time I distinctly heard Mr. Bowles's cock, next door, crow twice.

'There you are,' he said, rising and reaching for his hat; 'that's the sort of thing we have to put up with. What IS the time?'

I looked at my watch, and found it was half-past three.

'I thought as much,' he muttered. 'I'll wring that blessed bird's neck if I get hold of it.' And he prepared to go.

'If you can wait half a minute,' I said, getting out of bed, 'I'll go a bit of the way with you.'

'It's very good of you,' he rejoined, pausing, 'but it seems unkind to drag you out.'

'Not at all,' I replied; 'I shall like a walk.' And I partially dressed myself, and took my umbrella; and he put his arm through mine, and we went out together.

Just by the gate we met Jones, one of the local constables.

'Good-night, Jones,' I said (I always feel affable at Christmas-time).

'Good-night, sir,' answered the man a little gruffly, I thought. 'May I ask what you're a-doing of?'

'Oh, it's all right,' I responded, with a wave of my umbrella; 'I'm just seeing my friend part of the way home.'

He said, 'What friend?'

'Oh, ah, of course,' I laughed; 'I forgot. He's invisible to you. He is the ghost of the gentleman that killed the wait. I'm just going to the corner with him.'

'Ah, I don't think I would, if I was you, sir,' said Jones severely. 'If you take my advice, you'll say good-bye to your friend here, and go back indoors. Perhaps you are not aware that you are walking about with nothing on but a night-shirt and a pair of boots and an opera-hat. Where's your trousers?'

I did not like the man's manner at all. I said, 'Jones! I don't wish to have to report you, but it seems to me you've been drinking. My trousers are where a man's trousers ought to be—on his legs. I distinctly remember putting them on.'

'Well, you haven't got them on now,' he retorted.

'I beg your pardon,' I replied. 'I tell you I have; I think I ought to know.'

'I think so, too,' he answered, 'but you evidently don't. Now you come along indoors with me, and don't let's have any more of it.'

Uncle John came to the door at this point, having been awaked, I suppose, by the altercation; and, at the same moment, Aunt Maria appeared at the window in her nightcap.

I explained the constable's mistake to them, treating the matter as lightly as I could, so as not to get the man into trouble, and I turned for confirmation to the ghost.

He was gone! He had left me without a word—without even saying good-bye!

It struck me as so unkind, his having gone off in that way, that I burst into tears; and Uncle John came out, and led me back into the house.

On reaching my room, I discovered that Jones was right. I had not put on my trousers, after all. They were still hanging over the bed-rail. I suppose, in my anxiety not to keep the ghost waiting, I must have forgotten them.

Such are the plain facts of the case, out of which it must, doubtless, to the healthy, charitable mind appear impossible that calumny could spring.

But it has.

Persons—I say 'persons'—have professed themselves unable to understand the simple circumstances herein narrated, except in the light of explanations at once misleading and insulting. Slurs have been cast and aspersions made on me by those of my own flesh and blood.

But I bear no ill-feeling. I merely, as I have said, set forth this statement for the purpose of clearing my character from injurious suspicion.

MORE CHRISTMAS NIGHTMARES

Festive cheer turns to maddening fear in this new collection of seasonal hauntings, presenting the best Christmas ghost stories from the 1850s to the 1960s.

The traditional trappings of the holiday are turned upside down as restless spirits disrupt the merry games of the living, Christmas trees teem with spiteful pagan presences and the Devil himself treads the boards at the village pantomime.

As the cold night of winter closes in and the glow of the hearth begins to flicker and fade, the uninvited visitors gather in the dark in this distinctive assortment of haunting tales.

It is too often accepted that during the nineteenth and early twentieth centuries it was the male writers who developed and pushed the boundaries of the weird tale, with women writers following in their wake – but this is far from the truth.

This new anthology presents the thrilling work of just a handful of writers crucial to the evolution of the genre, and revives lost authors of the early pulp magazines with material from the abyssal depths of the British Library vaults returning to the light for the first time since its original publication.

Delve in to see the darker side of *The Secret Garden* author Frances Hodgson Burnett and the sensitively-drawn nightmares of Marie Corelli and May Sinclair. Hear the captivating voices of *Weird Tales* magazine contributors Sophie Wenzel Ellis and Greye La Spina, and bow down to the sensational and surreal imaginings of Alicia Ramsey and Leonora Carrington.

ALSO AVAILABLE

'But foliage surrounded him, branches blocked the way; the trees stood close and still; and the sun dipped that moment behind a great black cloud. The entire wood turned dark and silent. It watched him.'

Woods play a crucial and recurring role in horror, fantasy, the gothic and the weird. They are places in which strange things happen, where it is easy to lose your way. Supernatural creatures thrive in the thickets. Trees reach into underworlds of pagan myth and magic. Forests are full of ghosts.

Lining the path through this realm of folklore and fear are twelve stories from across Britain, telling tales of whispering voices and maddening sights from deep in the Yorkshire Dales to the ancient hills of Gwent and the eerie quiet of the forests of Dartmoor. Immerse yourself in this collection of classic tales celebrating the enduring power of our natural spaces to enthral and terrorise our senses.

ALSO AVAILABLE

*'Outside, where the air was foggy, the square was noiseless,
save for an occasional hoot of a motor passing into the
streets. By degrees I found the light growing rather dim,
as if the fog had penetrated into the room...'*

As the smoky dark sweeps across the capital, strange stories emerge from the night. A séance reveals a ghastly secret in the murk of Regent's Canal. From south of the Thames come chilling reports of a spring-heeled spectre, and in Stoke Newington rumours abound of an opening to another world among the quiet alleys.

Join Elizabeth Dearnley on this atmospheric tour through a shadowy London, a city which has long inspired writers of the weird and uncanny. Waiting in the hazy streets are eerie tales from Charlotte Riddell, Lettice Galbraith and Violet Hunt, along with haunting pieces by Virginia Woolf, Arthur Machen, Sam Selvon and many more.

British Library Tales of the Weird collects a thrilling array of uncanny storytelling, from the realms of gothic, supernatural and horror fiction. With stories ranging from the nineteenth century to the present day, this series revives long-lost material from the Library's vaults to thrill again alongside beloved classics of the weird fiction genre.

We welcome any suggestions, corrections or feedback you may have, and will aim to respond to all items addressed to the following:

The Editor (Tales of the Weird), British Library Publishing,
The British Library, 96 Euston Road, London NW1 2DB

We also welcome enquiries through our Twitter account, @BL_Publishing.